TAMA-RE

The Great Reawakening

Dr. Berkley 33°

Berk Entertainment

ISBN: 978-1-956174-06-9

Printed in the United States of America

First Printing, 2020

The Great Reawakening

-Begins-

CHAPTER 1

Because of the question, an elder
informs the inquisitive African
American visitors of a place where they
could journey and receive the
information that they are seeking,
which would cause them to have a mental
explosion, enlightening them to a world
forgotten by some, unknown to most.

When the unexpecting five African
American men arrived in Mali, they only
hoped to see the ancient ruins of the
University of Timbuktu. They never
expected to get the question answered.
Yet several days into the trip, their
tour guide introduces them to an elder
who promises to show them a mysterious
place. With excitement, they accept his
offer.

Immediately they leave for the
mysterious place. There is a slight
breeze. The night is unusually pleasant
as the cloudless sky shines with bright
stars aligning on this specific day.
The elder knows it is risky because no
African American has ever been in the
sacred space. But as the stars show, it
is time to transfer the knowledge to
outsiders of the tribe.

The elder sticks his hand into the sand. He digs a little way and pulls it out. He silently says, "it smells like gas. The water is near. This way." The elder begins walking faster. From what seems to be out of nowhere, 14 elders join them. They start to chant in an unfamiliar language, not the standard French or Arabic, as they walk towards a ruin resembling a small pyramid.

When they arrive, except for one of them, they light their kerosene lanterns, the other elder lights a torch, preparing to enter the pyramid. As they enter, their chant becomes piercing. The group encounters tunnels of different shapes and sizes. If not careful, they could go into the wrong one, losing valuable time and possibly their lives.

The elders know which tunnel will lead them to the correct room. They walk down the tunnel as the African Americans nervously look around. After several yards, they arrive at a large room on the right side and enter it. The group stands on a small half circle ledge. An elder places the torch on a circular structure that lights the entire room. An African American looks down. The only thing he sees is the surface of water more than 40 feet

below. The walls are rocks forming a
peculiar shape.

An elder motions his hand along the
path to its end, which leads to the
center of the room. In the center is an
altar with different relics on it.
Another elder points to the path. He is
instructing them to follow it to the
altar.

They, the African Americans, begin
to walk the path. When they reach the
altar, the room starts to shake. The 15
elders run out of the room, leaving the
African Americans in the room, not
knowing what to do. One yells, "we're
going to die!" Just at that moment, the
elder who led them to the pyramid
reenters. "We have to go, hurry." He
rushes them back through the pyramid
tunnels while asking for forgiveness.
They make it out of the pyramid.

The elder says, "I'm sorry. I must
go." He quickly leaves.

The men are confused about what just
happened. Glad to be alive, they hug
each other. The experience is something
they will never forget.

The next day, three of the men see
the elder. They stand over him while he
sits. He acts as if he does not

recognize them. Then he starts to speak, "I don't know what went wrong. There were 5 of you present, just like it read." He pauses, looking like he is losing his mind as he begins rubbing his head. "I seriously do not know what went wrong. All the signs were pointing to yesterday. But we have failed." The elder begins to weep.

"Shaikh, Shaikh," a young man wearing a white jalabiya and kufi runs up. He is holding a leather journal. He opens it. "Look here. The lesson you had me read today says the ritual must be down in a foreign but familiar place. Your calculation of the day was right, but the place was wrong."

The elder looks as he wipes the tears from his eyes. "We must find the place. And do the ritual there, but I'm old and things have become too expensive for us to travel." He looks at the three African Americans. "We need you to find the place." The elder waves his young student closer. "Give them the English translation of what we need."

The young student shows them the journal. The words are in classical Arabic. One of the men pulls out his working tools (a pen and paper). The student begins to translate classical Arabic into English.

The elder and the student walked off after he shows them. Never to be seen again.

CHAPTER 2

It is a cloudy night. The skyscrapers light up DOWNTOWN MILWAUKEE. A few miles away, nine people of different races are protesting. They all have a blue headband with Hebrew letters זָכַר written in yellow. The Hebrew word זָכַר is pronounced Zakar. It means to remember. They are wearing dark blue Dickies style jumpsuits. They march in a circle outside the café where Dr. Freeman is holding a lecture. The lecture is on the influence of Africans on the development of the west.

ROBERT, an African American in his 20s, is wearing a blue blazer with a button-down shirt without a tie. He wears khaki color jeans with a brown tweed belt. He is wearing blue Cole Haan shoes with a brown tongue and white soles. He walks towards the café. He looks at one of the signs that read, Anti-Semitism is a sin.

Just as he turns his head back in the direction he was going, he almost runs into a homeless man. Robert has seen him before, but something looks different. He appears to be weak from the lack of food or some disease. His face is abnormally thin even his hair lays matted under his dirty black winter hat. Except for dirt and pee-stains, his pants would be white except for dirty pee-stains. All the inner material is hanging out of his torn-up winter coat. He does not have shoestrings in either pair of his shoes, one torn in the front.

The HOMELESS MAN asks Robert, "Do you have a cigarette? Thoth, Thoth… Lake Michigan is his teachings."

Robert sarcastically replies, "WHAT?"

"As above; So below. Lake Michigan looks like the energy grid of the universe."

"That makes no sense. What's wrong with you? What's your name, sir, because you need some help?" Robert looks at the man. He thinks the man is totally out of his mind.

"RUSSELL; Russel equals 25 or 7. The mysteries. Grandmaster Russell." He looks at Robert and smiles. Then he slowly walks away.

Robert watches him walk. The man twitches and talks to himself. Robert shakes his head, then walks towards the front door of the café. He is there to hear Dr. Freeman's lecture. When he enters the cafe, a sign directs him to the second floor. He is late.

The host already introduced Dr. Freeman.

DR. FREEMAN, an African American master numerologist within his 70s whose face etched with deep wrinkles, stands at the podium. He is wearing a three-piece African Dashiki set with a matching hat. He has an Ankh necklace.

He puts his letter "J" shaped cane to the side. He rotates two gold pinky rings, one on each hand, as if performing a ritual. He grabs the PowerPoint clicker as he fidgets with it like a delicate man. When he speaks, he sounds powerful and friendly. "Thank you for the warm introduction." He pauses in a relaxed way. "Your welcome is much better than those upset people outside. I still laugh when they call me Anti-Semitic. I've been a Muslim for most of my life. Islam is a Semitic religion."

Some of the audience nervously laugh. Others laugh because they find it funny.

"Well, I do not want to waste any more of your time. Let's get into my presentation. New technology frustrates me." He still fumbles with the clicker. He finally pulls it together and goes to the first slide that reads, "WHY DIDN'T THE EUROPEANS ADAPT ISLAM?"

As Dr. Freeman analyzes the slide, he says, "let me give you a brief story about this question. I was 19 years old when a friend asked it. At the time, I didn't want to entertain the idea because of my Islamic faith. But he kept persisting. We took a trip to Mali in Africa to see the ruins of the University of Timbuktu.

My friend Russell asked one of our tour guides the same question. The tour guide told us about the Order of the Marrano.

Russell asked him if it still exists. The tour guide said he didn't know but offered to take us to an elder to ask."

When Robert hears the name Russell, he leans forward. He reflects on the homeless man he just encountered. He has become more attentive.

Dr. Freeman continues, "Russell, three more young men, and I were the only ones who visited the elder. To get the answer, we had to go through an initiation. After the initiation, we received the knowledge written on papyrus paper by the Egyptian Deity Thoth, who a few call Tehuti that had been a part of their culture for centuries."

Dr. Freeman goes to the next slide. It was a picture of Thoth. "I didn't know too much about Thoth."

Dr. Freeman describes the picture, "Tehuti or Thoth stands as a full human with an Ibis bird mask. He holds a quill as he writes the secrets of the universe on a papyrus tablet. During my studies, I found that Thoth was the Greek God Hermes whom most European mystics worship."

He looks over his glasses, expecting to see a flash of light from a person's aura, a sign written in the ancient prophecy. The prediction claims the dance of the magical lights would occur before the date of December 21st, 2012. According to his calculation, it should be today, Tuesday, May 15th, 2012. He did not see it the entire day, so he figures it will be in this small audience, but nothing happens.

He goes to the next slide, an image of EGYPTIAN PRIESTS. He explains, "here, the Egyptian Priests, as you can see, are black African males and females, which contradicts the European teachings of priests being male. In the picture, they are wearing black garbs. They wear a headdress called a namuz. They also wear a triangular shaped apron with Egyptian letters on it. They are looking at the writings of Tehuti. The priesthood is known for studying, negotiating, leading prayer, conducting rituals, advising rulers, and doing business. There also are claims found in several writings that the Greeks have used some of Tehuti's teachings in their mythological stories."

Dr. Freeman looks out into the audience again, still seeing nothing with a sigh, he clicks to the next slide that says MALI SCHOLARS. He describes the scholars, "they wear a white jalabiya. Some have a turban wrapped around their heads. Others wear black or red mini-fezzes.

They are in the UNIVERSITY OF TIMBUKTU. They are black scholars known as keepers of the temple who study, practice, and protect the sacred writings of Tehuti.

They teach anyone who comes for their counsel, if found worthy, they share the lessons from Tehuti's writings."

He has two more slides to see if his calculation is right. If an aura does not shine, he is wrong. He clicks to the next slide.

"The MARRANO."

Two flashes of light quickly show like an explosion. The only person who sees it is Dr. Freeman, correctly proving the lineage is in Milwaukee. He used both the Ahmose and Chaldean forms of numerology in his calculation. Milwaukee has nine letters that equal 37, the vowels equal 23, and consonants equal 14. According to the Chaldean explanation on the number 23, it represents the Royal Star of Leo, whereas the number 37 represents the Royal Star of the Bull known as the Aldebaran of Taurus or bull's eye. In the Orion Star Constellation, the Aldebaran star sits in the hand of Osiris, proving again that there is a high form of arcane energy in Milwaukee, Wisconsin.

The name Wisconsin has 9 letters, equaling the master number 44. The letters WIS or 5-9-1 reflect the

letters SIN or 1-9-5. Each set
represents Christ Consciousness. The
letters CON equal 14 which is the
foundation of Christ. Milwaukee,
Wisconsin has 18 letters which equal
the perfect reflection of 81, giving
off an intense occult energy.

But Dr. Freeman is confused, the
lights appear to be dancing. He
watches as they connect. Then they
violently disconnect. The prophecy did
not say this would happen. There was
only supposed to be one light. What was
going on? Was something wrong? Were
these opposing forces? He knew only
time would tell.

His entire demeanor changes to a
feeling of excitement. The slide of the
Marrano shows men and women wearing
black pants and a suit coat. They all
wear a black fez with a golden 6-
pointed star and crescent on the left
side.

A golden cape hangs from their
shoulders. Some wear a golden sash
while others wear an apron with golden
fringes. The cape has the same emblem
as the fez. Those who wear the apron
also have a golden chain around their
necks.

"In the days of what is now known as the Christian period, groups of Africans expanded their territory because most people of the land didn't accept the oldest way. The majority were traditionalists. They only wanted to practice their current way of life. So, the Marrano left the shores of Africa, taking the oldest practices with them.

Their entire purpose was to find a new place to rebirth and cultivate it. Even though it was the way of life of the old, it now would serve a larger purpose.

The laws of Tehuti were practiced by enforcing universal laws, rendering justice where the usual means were too slow or too uncertain. They were not Christian or Muslims but showed brotherly love and charity to the disbelievers of their way. They built upon a broader realm that receives all humans alike, but only if they believed in the Creative forces and are of good character which could pass the strictest of tests, qualifying them to gain membership in any order.

These African Marrano entered Europe after they instructed the black MOORISH soldiers to conquer the land and black BARBARY SAILORS to conquer the oceans.

14

They used the teachings of Tehuti that had been used for 13 hundred years, to govern all affairs. They also accompanied Christopher Columbus to the Americas. They set up different businesses needed to develop the land according to the writings of Tehuti.

Many men of high orders opposed them. They feared it would be of detriment to their Orders to which nothing could be added or taken away. So the Orders created an argument that says the Africans had nothing to do with them except sharing a higher knowledge capable of advancing any group of people on the planet, claiming the Marrano only theorized the teaching, they didn't practice them."

Dr. Freeman knew someone in the audience could be a part of his new mission. He just had to find out who. The answer would take a different type of calculation.

Since the aura appeared, he brought Russell back up, "Russell's question took on more life. It was no longer about the influence of the Black Islamic Moors. It was about the group most thought were the Black Hebrews expelled from Spain at the same time as the expulsion of the Black Islamic Moors."

He walks to the main computer and
fumbles with it, looking for another
slide presentation that goes further
into the explanation of the Marrano. He
finds it, clicking through the slides
until he gets to the right one. "Let me
explain a little more." The slide is
titled *Moors in different countries on
the European and Asian continents*. "My
research shows that there were several
groups of Africans in Europe from 700
A.D. to 1492 A.D. during the expulsion
of the Moors. As I already mentioned,
the groups were the Moors, Barbary, and
the Marrano. The Europeans received
information from the Marrano, which
they turned into what we now call the
Hebrew doctrine. Therefore, the
European monotheistic order of religion
is wrong. It is not Judaism,
Christianity, and Islam. It should be
Christianity, Islam, and Judaism. Now
you know why the group is outside
protesting."

After this information, he goes back
to the original slide presentation,
showing a different group of Africans.
"These are the OLMEC. They wear dark
close. They have a sword on their side.
They also carry a gun in their waist
belt. Their helmets are leather.

Some called them the Barbary
Sailors. Olmecs were in the Americas

before 1492 A.D. They warred with the European pirates for hundreds of years. They were the ones responsible for kidnapping Europeans as they traveled the ocean back and forth from America to Europe.

Initiated Olmecs received the sciences of Tehuti as well. Their duty was to hide the writings from the Europeans and the hired European pirates who attempted to steal them. The Europeans knew the teachings of Tehuti explains the many secrets of the universe. And they wanted them."

Although the lecture is still going, Robert gets up to utilize the bathroom. The bathroom is old and small. It has one urinal and one toilet. The tile on the walls is dingy, it looks like they have smoke damage. It makes the bathroom look unclean. The building has to be much older than he thinks. He pulls out his cellphone. He dials a number.

A male voice answers the phone, "Yes, may I help you?"

Robert responds, "What happened? You should be here. The professor is droppin some jewels."

"I hear you, RT, but something came up. I couldn't make it. Just take some notes and report back to base once things are over."

"I wish you would have been here. Your wisdom could have made sense out of all the things going on tonight."

"You have my instructions."

Robert disappointedly acknowledges the directive, "Yessir." He hangs up the phone and returns to the lecture.

When the lecture ends, the room is set up for people to ask Dr. Freeman questions. Microphones are on the outside of the rows and between the three sections of chairs.

A black woman with short hair wearing a black turtleneck sweater and gray slacks walks to the microphone holding a notebook and pen. "Dr. Freeman, my name is Professor Riley. I appreciate all the information you've shared. It somewhat aligns with my research interest. The question I have is: were all the different African groups a part of the same tribe?"

"That is an excellent question. It's hard to tell since we know that before Europeans kidnapped Africans, there

were over 2,000 different languages.
Meaning there may have been over 2,000
cultural practices.

Elders from different African
nations told me that the groups were a
mixture of warriors from all walks of
life and practices. They didn't
indicate if they were from the same
tribe. You still asked an exceptional
question."

Another woman wearing an Ankara wrap
African skirt along with a matching
headwrap waits at another microphone.
She asks, "Dr. Freeman, we always hear
about men's adventures. Were there
women involved?"

"Can we say mitochondrional DNA,
which is one of the powers women have
to transfer genes? Women are the first
teachers. They are the ones who chose
the leaders of several tribes. If we
think of Ancient Egypt, the so-called
queen is the one who permitted the king
to sit on the throne. Women are the
closest aligned to nature.

Women have always been heavily
involved in our affairs. Many times, we
fail because we don't include women. I
believe that a woman must always
accompany a man in leadership roles.
It's not only about balance. It's

harmony. Further, a woman and a man are needed to unlock the buried mysteries. We have to rewrite women back into our history."

"Dr. Freeman," a white man wearing blue jeans and a polo shirt walk to the outer left microphone to ask a question. "Dr. Freeman, thank you for coming and giving your highly informative speech. I have one question. What happened to Russell?"

"Well, the group that I am a part of decided to fund Russell, sending him on a mission to find out more information about his question. First, we sent him to Luxor in Egypt. Then we sent him to Mexico.

He never returned from Mexico. We didn't even receive a letter. So, we believe he may have lost his life."

Gasps spread around the room. Soon after the question-answer session is over, someone escorts Dr. Freeman to the first floor of the café. It is set up for him to autograph his books. The lecture expounds more on the book Robert read.

Dr. Freeman sits at a table as several people get their books autographed. Robert patiently waits his turn. When there's an opening, he approaches Dr. Freeman. "Dr. Freeman, I enjoyed your lecture."

"Thank you. I enjoyed giving it."

"I own a copy of your book but do not have it with me. I want to tell you what happened to me when I first got here."

"Make it quick. We have people still wanting to get their books signed."

"Yessir, well…" As he starts to speak, a woman stepped in to get her book signed.

She looks to be in her early 20s. But it is hard to tell her age because she looks like a sophisticated timeless hourglass. As the saying goes, 'Black, don't crack.'

She is wearing a tight fitted middie black dress. The dress is a little above her knees. It is rounded slightly under the bottom of her neck. She is wearing black thong sandals. She also is wearing a light layer of makeup and lip gloss. Her silky and straight hair is tied in a ponytail. The length hangs to the middle of her back. Dr. Freeman smiles as if he discovered a mystery.

The woman seductively expresses, "Thank you, Dr. Freeman. Could you sign my book?"

Dr. Freeman nods as if to say yes. "What's your name?"

"I'll spell it for you."

"Okay"

"M-I-S-C-H-E-L"

"Looks like it is pronounced Michelle?"

"No, it sounds like Mee-shell."

He begins signing the book.

She asserts, "You smell like Egyptian Musk, a man who knows the natural scent of body oil, I see.

"And you smell like Chanel." Dr. Freeman finishes signing the book and gives it back to her.

"I want to hear more about your experience. How can I do this?"

"Give me a second, ma'am. I want to hear what this young man has to say.

Mischel looks upset that he is blowing her off. But she continues to stand there waiting to get further information.

Dr. Freeman gestures Robert to come closer. Robert steps behind the table closer to Dr. Freeman's seat. "Oh, you have a Mason ring. My grandfather Rusty was a part of the brotherhood when he was alive."

"Your Grandfather must have been an important man since he was a member of the brotherhood. Back in the days, you had to be an influential part of your community." His demeanor changes when he finds out about Robert's grandfather. He becomes more open. Although Masons wear the same ring, he is not a Mason. But, it shows Robert pays attention to symbolism. "So, what did you want to tell me."

"When I arrived at your lecture, I was approached by a homeless man. He smelled bad, but that doesn't have anything to do with it," Robert laughs. "I asked him his name. He told me his name was Russell. So, when I heard you speak about a man named Russell, I wondered if he were the same person?"

"I do not know. Did Russell say anything else?"

"He said something about the number 7. He called himself a Grandmaster and the lake being an energy grid. None of it made sense to me."

Dr. Freeman seemed surprised, "Have you seen this man around here before?"

"Yes, I've seen him walking around talking to himself for years, but he looked different tonight."

"That is interesting. Have you heard of walk-ins?"

"NO, what's that?"

Dr. Freeman does not explain any further. "Well, what's your name?"

"Robert Turner, but my family calls me RT."

Dr. Freeman sits for a while. "Do you spell that R-O-B-E-R-T T-U-R-N-E-R?"

"Yessir."

"Is this your full name?" Dr. Freeman acts more interested in Robert.

"Yessir"

"You do not have a middle name?"

24

"No sir, just Robert Turner."

Dr. Freeman sits looking into space. He nods his head, "Interesting."

"What's interesting, sir?" Robert inquires.

"Your name. In fact, I'd like to invite you to a gathering that I'm having with some of my brothers tomorrow. Who knows, one of them might know your grandfather. Would you like to come?"

"Yessir, can I bring a close friend of mine?"

"Bring who you'd like. I trust you have good character judgment and will bring someone of high quality." Dr. Freeman writes down the location and time. "Here's the time and location. I'll see you tomorrow."

"Yessir, thank you."

They shake hands. Robert walks out of the door.

Mischel looks at Dr. Freeman with an attitude. She approaches him. "Do you have time now?"

"I definitely have time now. How can I assist you?"

"I heard so many good things about the great Dr. Lemuel Freeman. I want to hire you to explain somethings about me."

"I like money. Let's meet tomorrow morning back here for breakfast. I'll pay for the meal, and you can pay for my service."

"Sounds like you're trying to take me on a date."

"Not yet, but who knows what the future holds."

In the meantime, Robert walks towards his car. He takes his cellphone out and dials a number.

"Yes, may I help you?"

"Dr. Freeman invited me to meet with some of his brothers and him tomorrow. I asked him if I could bring someone. Are you available, tomorrow?"

"Yes, text me the information. I will pick you up." The phone hangs up.

He texts the information over, gets in his car, and drives off.

CHAPTER 3

The next morning Dr. Freeman arrived early at the café. He is wearing something like what he wore to his lecture. This time it was a 2-piece Dashiki with a matching hat.

The waitress greets Dr. Freeman, "Good morning, Good Doctor. You must can't stay away from us?"

"You know this is the best food in town."

"Well thank you, sir. Are you having the usual?"

"Yes, but I'm waiting for a possible client, so I'll wait until she gets here before I order. But you can bring some of your famous tea."

"Yessir, coming right up."

Dr. Freeman starts reading a book he recently purchased.

Mischel walks in, wearing a long shirt with black spandex. She greets everyone on the way to the table. She arrives at the table, hugs him, and says, "Dr. Freeman, how are you doing this morning? Wow, you're looking much younger than you did last night."

"I am doing my best. And you?"

"I woke up excited that I get to finally meet and have a one on one conversation with the man who healed many."

"They healed themselves. Like I healed myself to look younger this morning. I only gave instructions on what to do."

"I need those instructions."

The waitress comes back to the table with the tea. "Good morning, ma'am. Can I start you with something to drink?"

"Good morning. Could I have a glass of water, no ice?"

The waitress nods her head. Then she hands Mischel a menu. She walks off to get the water.

"So Mischel, you should look at the menu before we get started."

Mischel looks at the menu. The waitress comes back with the water. "Are the two of you ready to order?"

28

"I just need a few more minutes,"
Mischel responds. "Do you know what you
want, Dr. Freeman."

"Oh, yes, I get the same thing every
time."

Several people enter the restaurant,
seeming to know Dr. Freeman. They each
come and greet him, engaging in a short
conversation. Mischel finally is ready.

"Are you ready to order?"

"Yes"

Dr. Freeman gets the attention of
the waitress. She comes and takes their
orders.

"Before we get started, tell me a
little about yourself."

"I do not know where to begin."

Dr. Freeman jokingly replies,
"Usually people start at the beginning.
Tell me about your parents."

Mischel laughs, "Well, I have an
interesting story about them. My mother
raised me. I never met my father. But
my mother has told me the story of how
they met."

"Sounds interesting. Do tell."

"Are you sure?"

"Yeah, how else will I get to know how to help you? Or if we can work together."

Mischel agrees and begins to tell the story. For most of her life, she has kept it to herself, not even sharing it with people that she dated.

She felt this was the opportunity to get it off her chest. She was looking for answers. And felt Dr. Freeman was the one who could give them to her. "My father comes from a wealthy family. His name is Jesús Ziad. He used to get teased a lot. People would call him Jesus from the Bible. But his name is pronounced Hay-Zeus. My mother's name is Ashley Greene. She told me they met during a thunderstorm. They were in Washington, DC."

"Oh, that is a mystical place. This story's going to be good."

"My father was there because his father had a business meeting. He was trying to win a contract with the US government. My mother was there visiting family members.

A strong storm rolled in from out of
nowhere. My mother was standing under a
doorway.

She described the building as
decorated with Egyptian statues. My
father came running, trying to get out
of the rain. They shared the doorway
and began talking. She said it was love
at first sight."

"Do you believe in love at first
sight?"

"Not at all because they didn't
last."

"Okay, continue."

"My mother said they secretly spent
the next two weeks together. Both were
on their way to college after the
school year. They exchanged numbers
keeping in contact.

They planned to go to the same
college, and it worked because they
were both accepted. My father worked on
a business degree. His parents wanted
him to take over the family
construction business."

"And your mother?"

"She majored in Black Studies. She said that they were a hot item. The only problem was their parents didn't know about their relationship. After their sophomore year, my father wanted to take a trip to Spain. He learned about a co-op called Mondragon Corporation. The employees own the business."

"Ah, yes, I am very familiar with it," Dr. Freeman acknowledges.

"My grandfather unknowingly paid for my parents' trip. My mother fell in love with the cooperative idea. But my father questioned it. She claimed his love of capitalism began to show.

My mother got pregnant with me in Spain. She finished her junior year but decided to sit out her senior year to take care of me. My father continued his degree work."

"Did your mother complete her degree?"

"No."

"Why not?"

"Well, they began to argue a lot about socialism and capitalism. My mother knew she wouldn't be able to live with his capitalist ideas. Although she loved him, she was looking for an opportunity to leave him."

"So how did she pull it off?"

"Even though they were living together, their parents still didn't know about their relationship. My mother's parents knew about me but didn't know who my father was.

My father knew, if he told his parents about his relationship, they would disown him, but he vowed to let it happen. My mother refused to let it happen one day, she packed our things and left, cutting all communications with my father. She didn't even tell him that her family relocated to another state during their sophomore year. There was no way he was going to find us."

Dr. Freeman was concerned with her mental state. "How does that make you feel?"

"In all honesty, I feel like an abandoned child without a father. I've mistreated men, or they mistreated me in every romantic relationship I've been in, and I think that my father not being in my life is the cause."

"I can understand," Dr. Freeman compassionately replied.

The waitress comes with their food. She places it in front of them. "Would you like anything else?"

"Nothing for now," Mischel replied.

"Everything is perfect as usual," Dr. Freeman answered.

"If y'all need anything, let me know." She walks off.

Dr. Freeman takes out a piece of paper and a pen. He pushes it towards Mischel. "Write your maiden name, include your middle name on the paper, and your full birthdate."

She wrote Mischel Ziad and her birthdate.

"You do not have a middle name?"

"No"

Dr. Freeman begins calculating her name. According to your last name, you come from a family of magicians. They probably did very well in business. I wouldn't be surprised if your grandfather won the contract. Your first name shows that you should be teaching master lessons because you can be a proficient teacher. You can show people how to create new paths for their lives. You're an innovator of some sort."

Mischel grabbed her chest, "Really?"

"Oh yes, if you use the flow of energy right, the world could benefit from what you have to offer.

CHAPTER 4

Later that afternoon, Dr. Freeman is talking to MARC WILLIAMS, NATHAN LEWIS, and JACOB MOLETREE about Russell. They are all around the same age.

Marc Williams is a retired politician who is tall and has a bald head with no facial hair. While leaning back in his chair, he has a potbelly as if he had way too many beers.

Nathan Lewis spent most of his years working in the banking industry. His face etched with fine wrinkles, having a perfectly trimmed mustache, gold tee, and bald head. He is thin and a few inches shorter than Marc.

Jacob Moletree, a retired police officer, is short. Despite his lack of stature, he has a hint of authority as one who demands respect and receives it. He wears his hair in a military-style haircut with no facial hair. He is jittery like he is on some drugs.

They meet in the conference room, complete with original book matched mahogany paneling, fireplace, boardroom table, nine chairs, and a bookshelf with books as old as one hundred fifty years.

"I thought we destroyed his spirit," Jacob asks.

Dr. Freeman is puzzled. He reveals his confusion. "I still do not understand why you wanted to destroy his spirit. You were close friends."

Jacob states, "He lost his mind. He put our order in a bad position."

Dr. Freeman gets up to open the door at 3 P.M., the time he told Robert to arrive. If there, he could enter the sacred space. Dr. Freeman walks out as Robert stands while his friend remains seated.

"Good, you made it. Come in."

Robert and his friend walk past the two lion statues on each side of the door.

Dr. Freeman announces, "Robert…"

Robert looks nervous. "Please call me RT."

"Very well, RT, these are my brothers. Jacob Moletree is our Sovereign Grand Priest. Marc Williams

is our Lieutenant Sovereign Grand
Priest. Finally, this is Nathan Lewis.
He is our Sovereign Grand Treasurer,
and I'm the Sovereign Grand Historian."

"Hello gentlemen, this is the leader
of my family, CUE."

"Thank you for joining us, Cue. RT
highly recommends you." Dr. Freeman
welcomes Cue with a handshake.

Cue replies, "thank you for letting
me come with RT."

Dr. Freeman begins to explain the
reason for the invitation. "We are in
an extremely critical day and time. I
invited you because Robert, excuse me
RT, told me his grandfather was a
Mason. In our order, we pass our
knowledge down. And, I felt RT would be
a good person to pass it to."

Cue, while looking intense at Dr.
Freeman, is short but muscular, wearing
his hair in long braids.

Marc notices Cue's intense look,
"you're looking profoundly serious,
Cue. Do you have something on your
mind?"

"Yes, since you are all such
influential men of our community, I

want to know what you are going to do about the brother who got killed by the police last night? Rumor has it he was shot 7 times in the back while trying to get into a car door."

"We will wait to find out if there was any foul play, then the proper authorities will be contacted," Nathan replies.

"7 times while getting in a door, that's interesting," Dr. Freeman softly states.

Cue upsettingly implies, "that's exactly why we can't trust old men like you. You are all talk and no action. Wait, wait for what? So more black people get killed by the scums."

"Everything is a process, brother." Dr. Freeman attempts to justify why they must wait.

"Sounds more like an excuse than a process."

Jacob firmly interrupts, "I agree with you, Cue. The only way people listen is because of action. Especially action done against what they find valuable."

Cue nods his head in agreement. Robert sits silently, observing what is happening.

"I like the way you think." Jacob pulls out a business card from his pocket. He hands it to Cue. "If you want some advice on what exactly are vital points in this city that will shake things up, contact me."

Dr. Freeman replies, "as you can see, we all do not think alike. The numbers show…"

Jacob agitatedly responds, "if we aren't talking about numbers involving money, I do not want to hear it."

"It is not the right time," Dr. Freeman continues.

"Young brother, you have the energy to change the world. We are old and washed up. Do what you think needs to happen. You have my support."

Cue gets up from his chair. "It was nice meeting you, but business calls. We must plan our next move. I'm glad one of you understands." He looks at Jacob as if their souls are connected. "Let's go RT."

Robert reluctantly gets out of his seat. "Thank you, elders, for your time. I do appreciate it."

They leave the room.

CHAPTER 5

After Cue and Robert exit the room,
Jacob invites Dr. Freeman to his
office, where he systematically
displays his certifications of
accomplishments, which includes a large
leadership certificate from their
brotherhood. The office has a large
brown desk with two computer screens
and a chair. Behind his desk is a
cabinet built into the wall with space
where a flat-screen T.V. neatly sits.
Across from the desk, on the opposite
wall, is a recliner chair with two
large plants on each side. On one side
of the room is a couch, and directly
across from it is a liquor cabinet.

"Dr. Freeman, would you like a
drink?"

"What do you have?"

Jacob proudly walks to the liquor
cabinet. "I have Rémy Martin Louis XIII
Cognac for special occasions."

"You have expensive taste. How much
did that cost? $2,000."

"I bought this bottle for just under $4,000."

"What do you have for less special occasions? My taste buds aren't ready for $4,000 liquor."

Jacob laughs, "I have some Hennessy or some d'Usse Cognac VSOP. I know you love your cognac."

"I'll have some d'Usse Cognac VSOP, thank you."

"On the rocks?"

"No, straight."

Jacob pours a glass of liquor for Dr. Freeman and himself. At the same time, he speaks. "We've been friends for a long time."

Dr. Freeman sits with a disturbed look, not knowing why Jacob makes that unusual comment. It seems like he's up to something, so Dr. Freeman patiently waits to find out the purpose.

Jacob hands the drink to Dr. Freeman, who is sitting in the recliner. Jacob comments, "we should be in agreeance more when we have company."

"Jacob, yes, we have been friends for quite sometimes. Yet, I do not believe that we have to agree on everything."

"When we have company, I think we should not show division."

"You're right I'll work on that for the next time."

"Good… I have some good news. I think I found someone who will fund your research in Mexico."

"Really?" Dr. Freeman is surprised.

The last time they talked about his research, Jacob said it cost too much, claiming it was a bad idea and wanting to scrap the project. "Yes, the representative should be here in a few minutes."

They continue to chat while enjoying a few more drinks.

The phone rings, Jacob picks it up. "Send him in, thank you." Jacob hangs up the phone, simultaneously standing up as the door opens. An older tall white man with gray hair wearing a dark 3-piece suit enters. Jacob warmly greets the man, "ah, GEORGE GARDNER, double G, it has been a long time. Have a seat."

"Jacob, the traveling man. Yes, it has been a long time since we last saw each other at the joint session. I do not plan on staying long, so I'll stand."

"George let me introduce you to Dr. Freeman. He is our profound scholar on Black History."

"Please to meet you, brother," says George.

Dr. Freeman gets out of the recliner and walks over to shake his hand while replying, "the pleasure's mine."

"George and I both started on the force at the same time. We became friends when we learned that both of us were Masons. Back then white and black Masons didn't communicate."

George nods his head, affirming the statement and says, "except for us."

"Yeah, we had a different kind of bond. George helped me in my studies to understand the craft."

Dr. Freeman attempts to look impressed, but he is extremely

skeptical of their bond. He knows Jacob is an opportunist, always feeling that Jacob would throw his mother under a bus if money or power were on the table. Examining George, Dr. Freeman feels something is not quite right because he is remarkably pleasant for a white man. White men tend to be overly aggressive, being the worse type of opportunists. They will wait for generations to make a move, and even raise their children with the idea of conquering and staying in power. Yet, their relationship makes sense to Dr. Freeman.

Jacob curiously asks, "buddy, what have you been up to?"

"After retirement, I've just been traveling the world."

"Any place interesting?"

"My favorite place was Scotland, where I learned more about the connection between Masonry, Scotland, and the Scottish Rite. I'm working on a book about it as we speak."

"Oh, I learned a connection between Africans, Scotland, and the Masons, myself. I would like to read your book. When is the release date?" Dr. Freeman

46

comments to see if his assumption of George was right.

Scotland and England practiced Masonry differently. He learned how Scotland had been at war with England, an ally of France, for many years. The difference in the practices was due to the Knights Templar, persecuted in France subsequently, finding refuge in Scotland taking the esoteric knowledge they obtained from the Africans with them. Early England Masonry lacked higher knowledge, unlike Scotland.

George looks a little disgusted that Dr. Freeman brought up African involvement with Masonry and Scotland.

His assumption was right. George has a hint of racism.

"I do not have a release date. But let's get to why I'm here, Dr. Freeman."

Jacob starts looking concerned. He knows both Dr. Freeman and George are prideful of their beliefs.

"I have some very wealthy friends who are interested in the scroll you think is hidden in the pyramids in Mexico.

Dr. Freeman, many people may think you're crazy talking about some mythological scroll. But you, my Priest of Aaron friends, and I know the scroll is real."

Dr. Freeman looks at Jacob in disbelief. The only ones who were supposed to know about the scroll being in Mexico were their brotherhood. Everyone else was just supposed to think his interest in Mexico was the Olmec civilization, not the actual scroll. He already explained to Jacob what would happen if the Aaronites got a hold of the scroll. Why would he involve them? The saying is true. If you tell a person not to do something, it is human nature that they are more likely to do it.

The name Aaronites, short for the Brotherhood of Aaron, whose members called themselves Priest of Aaron, derives from the story of Moses and Aaron in the Bible. Moses was the prophet, but since he had a speech impediment, God appointed his brother, Aaron, to speak, eventually making him the lead priest for the Israelites, which had two priesthoods. The family of Aaron was one group, and the tribe of Levi was the other group known as the Levitical Priesthood.

The Brotherhood of Aaron believed Aaron was a master magician. When using numerology, the name Aaron equals 22. The number 22 is the master builder, and in some esoteric circles, it means the master magician. Aaron proved to be a master of words, each word having a unique vibration. Thus, the proper use of words can create miracles that appear to be magic.

The Brotherhood of Aaron used the hermetic principles found in the Kybalion and Kabballah. They often used the King James Version Bible to justify why they held so much power.

A rumor leaked from the Aaronites claiming that the most powerful, Aaronite of the 20th century, was born June 6, 1966, in New York. Since the child was unknown, people named him Aaron. When he turned 13 years old, a celebration occurred in America, marking the year by calling it *The Year of the Child*. The story continues to say Aaron became a Tech giant, operating a computer that held the personal information of everyone in the world. With this type of power, the child grew to control the very fabric of the world.

According to his birthday, he would turn 54 in 2020. There would be a giant celebration making his entrance into the last stage of his life. It begins at the age of 55. Initiates of the science of numerology were predicting that the celebration would last for 2 years starting in 2020 because the year 1966 adds to 22. They expected the markets to crash, the first year. The second year, they expected problems that involved air like airplane crashes, lung diseases, and telecommunication disruptions. The Aaronites were preparing for the event, which would put them back in power.

Jacob quickly interrupts. "I think we may have some young brothers who will be a good fit for the expedition to Mexico. We met with them a few hours ago."

Dr. Freeman, already in disbelief that Jacob would involve the Aaronites, becomes further disavowed with Jacob offering to put their lives at risk with something like this.

"Good, a lot is riding on the deal I made." George treats Jacob like he is less than him. "We're depending on your team and you to make it happen. Jacob, I hope I can count on you?"

"I won't let you down."

George looks at Dr. Freeman with a stare of an assassin, knowing Dr. Freeman will be a problem. Dr. Freeman returns the look. George does not say another word, walking out of the room as if he is disgusted that he was dealing with black men.

Dr. Freeman falls into the recliner chair, realizing their lives are in danger. "What was that? Jacob, what type of deal did you make?"

"Don't worry about it. We're all good. I have control over George. He is a killer, but he is not the smartest person in the world. Let's just get the scroll."

"I think you're underestimating him. He is well connected with the Aaronites," Dr. Freeman rebuttals.

CHAPTER 6

Cue is sitting on his couch, his three mates, JAZMINE, NEFER, and EBONY, are all in the room. His mates are all younger than him. He believes that when a man plans to make a woman his counterpart, she should be half his age plus nine years. Therefore, if a man is 50, his mate should be 34. If a man is 22, his mate should be 20.

Jazmine's body is like an hourglass standing about 5 feet 7 inches. Her skin is a golden-brown complexion. She has slanted eyes, which causes some people to say she looks like a black China doll. Her silky black hair is long. It touches the bottom of her back.

Nefer is about 5 feet tall. Her skin complexion is dark caramel brown. She wears her hair in a natural.

Ebony is slightly taller than Nefer. Her skin complexion is between Jazmine and Nefer.

Cue's top four generals are present. Robert is with his mate DIAMOND.

Nasir is with his mate, MARYUM. He is a tall, dark skin man with dreadlocks, a mustache, and a beard. She is light skin with lots. She is short and slender. She wears glasses.

CHANOKH and his mate, MEKA, are present. He is African and has a strong African accent. Meka is dark skin with a rounded shape face and wears her hair short.

Khufu is with his mate, STAR. He is brown skin with a mustache and a beard. He wears glasses. Star is a short caramel complexion woman who wears her hair in braids.

Everyone is in a black casual outfit.

Cue starts talking, "has anything new happen since our last meeting? Any new thoughts?" He attempts to be fair, but he knows he is always the one with the final word.

"I've been thinking about this socialism thing we spoke about several months ago," Khufu replies. "What have you come up with?"

"I'm thinking about how to develop our communities. The problem I keep running into is history shows how 100s of thousands of people lost their lives fighting for the utopian idea of socialism, which morphed into communism. I've been questioning myself if socialism is worth it at all?"

Chanokh chimes in, "I think if socialism is set up right, people can avoid all the bloodshed. Think about it. We all will be entitled to the same thing."

"Do you think white people want the same things we have? They have their white privilege." Nasir does not believe Chanokh would even think about equality with white people.

Chanokh optimistically says, "There are some white people who do not want much out of life but to love all humanity. I think the journey for love will outweigh anything else."

Nasir explains his position further. "Most of those same white people don't care about our oppression. They have a competitive hatred for their people who worked harder and have more than them.

Think about white people who protested the last time. Do they really give a damn about us? They just hate the rich white people and took the opportunity to express it by destroying businesses. Then the media blamed everything on black people."

Khufu continues the original thought, "when I was thinking about socialism, I started questioning why poor white people support the Republican Party."

Cue steps in, "so What did you come up with Khufu?" He wanted the others to listen to Khufu's position.

"The poor Republicans are caught in the hierarchy concept. The concept was mostly learned in their homes where their fathers ruled without question. So, who is ever in charge claiming the same believes as them, they will follow without question."

"Coming from Africa and studying in your universities, the thing I found interesting is how dangerous poor white people are who understand that they have white privilege but believe the system is treating them unequally.

They will join any cause to go against those who they feel are responsible for their unjust treatment." Chanokh seemed to have changed his position on white people after Khufu explained his thought.

Robert seems not to be interested in the conversation. He was focusing more on the esoteric meaning of things lately and wanted to know how to align with the energy forces. Robert already made his belief known. He believes money in the economy, regardless of the practice, is a form of energy used in the physical form to show a person's worth. It's earned and spent like the tide that ebbs and flows twice in 24 hours. In other words, it spins (spends) in a circular motion. He felt the generals had the wrong concern. "This is off subject, but I was thinking of how books and other writings are the opening of a vortex to the ultimate mind."

The other generals are annoyed as if Robert seems to always get off the subject. The sisters sit silently, not knowing what to think about Robert's statement as they wait to see if Cue would explain it further.

Robert continues, "I've been taking on a mental journey of how Romans built buildings which mostly do not stand, and other Europeans wrote books which are still around. But even more powerful and older is the Egyptians buildings and writings on the walls that still exist. The Egyptians undoubtedly are much more superior. I

question how? And why have so many
worked so hard to deconstruct their
greatness to the point of near
annihilation?"

Cue looks as if he has awakened to
the reason why Robert is interested in
Dr. Freeman. He must derail Robert's
interest. Cue is striving to be the
most powerful Black man in Milwaukee.
"All the ideas are very interesting,
but we have some pressing business that
we need to attend too. Men, let's meet
in the ceremony room.

Ladies, why don't you make plans for
the doula class. We want to bloom other
women in our community into their
fullness. We have to get back to when
men were warriors, and women were
Goddesses."

The brothers leave their mates and
enter the ceremony room. They all take
a seat in their designated place.

"It was nice meeting with the elders
today, but they are as useless to us as
the local politicians." Cue looks at
Robert to let him know that he does not
approve of the brothers.

Robert sits still and says nothing.
Cue gets out of his seat and begins
walking around the room. "So, we're

going to make our move tonight. Since the police want to kill unarmed brothers, and they don't police their own. We will take matters in our own hands.

I want all of you to get your people to tear the city up. Burn it down if they have to.

We will focus on businesses owned by white people, Arabs, Asians, and people from India. Don't touch the black businesses. I don't want our sisters or children in the streets. We don't have control over the other sisters and children yet, so they aren't our concern for now.

In the morning, I want our ladies to get out in the streets and start spreading the word that black people need to get out and vote.

We need to show our faces too. So, we will go to certain media outlets and talk about building up the black communities. We will demand that money comes to black communities. Any questions?"

Robert chimes in, "I think we should listen to Dr. Freeman. His work is thorough."

"The doctor is a charlatan. If we listen to anyone, it will be Mr. Moletree."

"Something didn't feel right about him. I don't feel he has our best interest," warns Robert.

"Who runs this family? Me or you?" Cue knows he needs Robert on his team. Because he is his top general, he calls him RT. It is a way to hide his identity and shows his position like stars show a general in the military rank. He has advanced beyond the other generals in knowledge and understanding. Cue uses the tactic to put fear in Robert's mind.

Robert sheepishly replies, "you do."

"Exactly, I already spoke with Mr. Moletree. He gave me some valuable information about the vital parts of the city that will affect the powers-that-be. But if you have a problem. I invite you to leave.

Robert begins to look off into space. Cue displays one of the leadership qualities that Robert does not like, along with being closed-minded. He looks at Robert for about a minute.

Robert waits a little longer. He gets up and walks out the door.

Cue yells so everyone can hear him, "if you walk out the door, there's no need to come back. You've committed treason in my eyes."

Robert keeps walking. He enters the living room where Diamond is sitting with the other sisters. They are in deep conversation. They did not even hear Cue. "Let's go Diamond."

Diamond is a slender, perfectly proportioned black woman who wears her long curly hair, in its natural style.

Performing in Luxembourg while he was on his world tour, at the time, having several big hit rap songs, Cue met Diamond. Diamond was one of the people who vocally commented about her appreciation. Cue developed a unique system after studying each country's culture, to relate to the audience by doing different things in each place. The idea was for the local citizens to keep their attention on him, noticing his effort, they appreciated him.

When they met, he was already dating several women. They occupied his house while he was on tour. He told the women about Diamond. That year on his birthday, the women came together and gave Cue a birthday gift. They surprisingly flew Diamond to Milwaukee to spend a few weeks with Cue. He gave her the name Diamond because he felt that she was a gem who would always be close to his heart.

Cue and Diamond could have been a hot item, but Diamond was not into sharing Cue with the other women. He knew this, as she unsuccessfully attempted to break Cue away from the women. Still infatuated with her, he moved her into his domain, even though she was not one of his women. Every so often, they would spend quality time together, but she still refused to budge from her refusal to share Cue.

Cue saw how people were attracted to him, mainly because of his music. He created a group called "The Family." His idea was to be an influential part of the city, eventually getting into politics, business, health care, and other aspects before he wanted to be the most powerful black man. Cue taught a mixture of religious practices, developing a religion he called *THE WAY*. When Robert joined The Family, Cue liked his enthusiasm, hooking him up with Diamond. He knew Diamond would keep a close watch on Robert because of her loyalty to him. Robert had no clue of their history.

Diamond hesitated, "What are you doing?"

"Leaving," Robert walks out Cue's house.

Diamond follows as her irritation mounts. "Have you lost your mind?"

"No, I have found it."

"You walked out on Cue. The man who made you who you are. I knew I should have joined his family instead of letting him convince me to be with you."

"What?"

"You heard me. You're weak. The sisters were right. You ain't no real man like Cue. You're his flunky. You are nothing without him.

I let my ego get in the way and didn't want to share a man. But he is all man. I knew it when he first brought me to America. He is fair and has always treated me right."

Robert nods his head in disgust. He begins to get angry but controls his emotions.

"I'm not going anywhere with you," sarcastically remarks Diamond.

"Okay!"

Diamond walks back into the house and slams the door.

Robert uncertainly walks with his head down, beginning to question if he made the right decision. Eventually, the fact is accepted, raising his head and walking off with a new sense of pride. But how long will this new pride last?

CHAPTER 7

The next morning Robert wakes up early, looking at his cellphone, the news reads that the city is chaotic, he believes Cue started the full-fledged uprising. During the night, it further reads, several people arrested, police officers and firefighters injured, buildings burning, so the mayor has issued a curfew.

At 7 am, Robert arrives at the three-story building called the Africology House that Dr. Freeman invited him to, but no one is in the building. The building is white with a symbol on a large sign. It reminds Robert of an acute triangle on its side attached to the bottom part of an Egyptian Ankh. The name AFRICOLOGY HOUSE, *dedicated to the study of Africa and its Diaspora,* is on the sign under the symbol. There are two large lions in the front, between the building and two lions (one facing east, and the other facing west) is a pillar with a globe on top. He decides to wait and sits on the steps between two large lions.

Several minutes pass until Dr. Freeman walks up. "Good morning, RT. What are you doing here?"

"You can call me Robert, sir."

"Okay Robert, you know I'm an old man. I can't keep up with all these name changes. What's going on? Why are you here?"

"Can we talk, sir?"

"Sure, I have a few minutes."

Dr. Freeman unlocks the front door. "Come inside."

Robert follows Dr. Freeman in the building. "I refused to do what Cue wanted."

"Good for you."

"What do you mean good for me?" Robert frustratingly asks. "My girlfriend left me because of it. It is over for me. I found out that she has a thing for Cue. I will never get respect in my community or The Family again."

"Interesting... most women do have a thing for men in power positions. And just because men are in leadership positions, doesn't mean they are leaders." Dr. Freeman looks at a man in despair. "Let me show you something. Follow me."

Robert follows Dr. Freeman in a room sectioned off into three stations. Each station has a desk. One of the desks is above a flight of 3 stairs. The other two desks are on the floor.

"Look around, this is the room every Mason including your grandfather has walked through. The problem is after they walk through it, they usually stop learning. They can't see the hidden lessons sitting in plain sight."

Robert looks around. He has no clue what it is. "Is this building a Mason building?"

"No, but we have the members of our brotherhood perform the first three degrees which every Mason performs."

"So, what exactly are you? This?"

"We are the Sovereign Order of the Mystic Priests of the Marrano."

"I never heard of it."

"That is not surprising. Most people haven't. They automatically assume we are Masons." Dr. Freeman hands him a notebook and pen. "You should take some notes. They may come in handy one day."

Robert excitingly follows the instructions. He is so excited that he seems to have forgotten about Cue, Diamond, and The Family.

"Our order gave the Europeans 2 degrees. In Masonry, they are known as the Entered Apprentice and Fellow Craft degrees. This was enough information needed to elevate each member to their highest self."

"Is this how the Europeans excelled to dominate the world?"

"They excelled because they not only utilized the principles, but they turned it on their fellow man. Therefore, you see only a very few people, in European history, in leadership positions of either king, queen, noble, or clergy."

"If this is the case, it makes sense."

Dr. Freeman expounds further, "Many orders like the Masons were developed back in those days. They even created colleges with the same structure. A good example is Cambridge University which started with 2 degrees. The bachelor's focused on Rhetoric, Grammar, and Logic. The master's focused on Geometry, Music, Arithmetic, and Astronomy."

"So, they pretty much had 7 courses?"

"Not necessarily 7 courses because it is possible to explain each area in several ways. Therefore, they had 7 areas of study, which can take more than a lifetime to learn."

"But they have so much more now."

"It seems that way," Dr. Freeman confirms. "The reality is: they have confused the basics so much that people have lost the technique to elevate to their higher selves."

Robert shakes his head, "Can it still be done? Can we still elevate ourselves?"

"Yes, with the right tools." Dr. Freeman points around the room. "There are four points each Mason passes, the north, south, east, and west. One of the things they represent is the four elements, air, water, fire, and earth. Most people only focus on the physical aspect of things. They do not look for the soul of things."

"The soul of things."

"Yes, people usually call it the spirit of things."

"Oh yes, we speak about that often in The Family. Cue has written literature explaining the spirit and four elements and speaks a lot about astrology. He has done each of our astrological charts. It is a little too complicated for me. So, I leave it alone."

"Yes, astrology is very complicated. I feel the same way. Because of its popularity, people tend to skip over the other three sciences. They do not realize that it is the fourth and last science. Astrology is the esoteric or feminine principle. Astronomy is the exoteric or masculine principle. If you are not personally following the physical movement of heavenly bodies, you're not doing astrology.

I focus on the first science myself, which is arithmetic, currently known as numerology. I deal with numbers."

"Numerology?"

"Yes," Dr. Freeman replies.

"Don't you think it should be called Numberology instead of numerology?"

Dr. Freeman laughs, "clever, but no, it's numerology. We can understand things using number systems. I use the 9-number system to read things such as words in the English language. Each letter in the English alphabet aligns with a number.

But let's get back to the room. In the center of the four points is an altar. On the altar, things of importance like the Holy Bible are placed."

"The bible is filled with contradictions. It is what the white man used to enslave us. It is a lie."

Dr. Freeman agrees, "it was used to enslave some of us especially the uninitiated because of its power. The coding must be known to understand the meaning."

"Code? Hold up Dr. Freeman, you really don't think that it is coded, do you?"

"Yes, do you remember Russell speaking about Thoth?"

"Yes."

"Thoth is the Egyptian Deity whom the European mystics call Hermes." Dr. Freeman picks up the Bible sitting on the altar. "The King James Version of the Holy Bible was translated by 46 people. One was Sir Frances Bacon also known as William Shakespeare."

"Do you mean Shakespeare, as in the poet?"

"Exactly, it has been claimed that Shakespeare's poems were written by an African woman named Amelia Bassano. Don't believe me, research it." Dr. Freeman pauses, then continues to say, "this means some of the translators of the bible were African." He looks at Robert.

Robert looks shocked.

Dr. Freeman then opens the Bible to Genesis. "Genesis using the numerology system equals 33. G is 7, E is 5, N is 5, E is 5, S is 1, I is 9, and S is 1. When they are added all together, they equal 33. The number 33 is the number for a master teacher or a master lesson."

"That is interesting because Jesus was crucified at the age of 33."

"Exactly, so his age must mean something else. Let's go to Genesis 1:1. I want you to count 33 verses from here and tell me what you get."

Robert begins counting. He stops. "Counting 33 verses down, I got Genesis 2:2."

"Read it."

Robert begins to read the verse, "And on the seventh day God ended his work."

Dr. Freeman interrupts him, "On what day?"

"Seventh."

"Thoth whom the Greeks call Hermes teaches 7 laws according to European teachings. The 33 verses alert us that a master lesson follows, which is the 7 mysterious but constant laws. In numerology, the number 7 represents the mysteries. Now go to Psalms 46."

Robert turns to Psalms 46.

"Have you heard about the name Shakespeare hidden in this verse?

"Yes."

"Explain it to me."

"There were 46 translators of the King James Version Bible. If you count 46 words down from the top, you see the word shake. And if you count 46 English words up from the bottom, you get spear. But my problem was always there are 47 words."

"That's a good problem to have. The number 47 added together equals 11. It's a master number. It can also mean some type of initiation which includes the use of pillars. We'll talk more about it some other time. Now go to Genesis 1:27."

Robert flips back to Genesis. He sees it and begins reading. "So, God created man in his own image, in the image of God created he him; male and female created he them."

"Is God a male or a female?"

"A male of course."

"Well, the Hebrew word for man is "awdam" which means human. If you look closely at this verse, you can see there are distinct differences between a male and a man.

Do you know the name for a human with both male and female genders?"

"A Hermaphrodite."

"Right," Dr. Freeman walks to a whiteboard. He writes the word Hermaphrodite. Then he writes Herm-aphro-dite under it. He writes Herm= Hermes; Aphro or Afro = African; dite = deity. Finally, he writes Hermes, the African Deity who is Thoth. "That is enough of the Bible for now. I need to go exercise. You can come with me if you'd like. I'm going to the lake."

"Yes, I need to get rid of some stress."

"Take a couple of minutes and write down what I explained. I have to get something. I'll be right back." Dr. Freeman leaves the room. He goes and starts up a computer to make some copies. He returns to the room. While he is gone, Robert writes down everything he can remember.

"Are you ready?"

"Yessir."

Robert follows Dr. Freeman out of the building. Dr. Freeman turns and locks the door. Then they get in Dr.

Freeman's car and drive to Lake
Michigan.

CHAPTER 8

On the way to Lake Michigan, Dr. Freeman expresses, "Robert, let me tell you what I think is the most important part of a person."

"What's that, Dr. Freeman?"

"The person's soul! The soul is different streams of energy bound together into a large mass like the sun in the center of our galaxy. Planets revolve around the sun, vibrating at various rates of speed based on their proximity to it. In numerology, the same thing occurs, numbers vibrate at different speeds. We can tell a lot about a person by reading their soul number. We further understand their past, present, and future actions because of the collaboration of vibrations ejecting from the other numbers, attaching to the soul number."

Robert looks off into the distance. He has nothing to say, at first. All he does is ponder on what Dr. Freeman told him. A few minutes pass before he asks, "If this is the case, can we help people, today?"

"Why yes, the most trouble-free and valuable information you can obtain is a person's birth date. The birthday alone gives you a large amount of information."

They arrive at Lake Michigan. The Africology House is approximately 10 minutes away. When they get out of the car, they see a black woman sitting on an arch shape cement wall. The design on the ground looks like a doorway, window, or an eye with an arc over it. As they walk towards the water, the woman recognizes Dr. Freeman.

"Dr. Freeman, I didn't think you were coming. I was starting to get disappointed," Mischel says with a slight attitude.

Dr. Freeman reaches to shake Mischel's hand.

"I'm a hugger. I do not shake hands." Mischel walks over to hug Dr. Freeman. She gives him a sensual hug.

Dr. Freeman politely pulls himself away. He is disturbed but understands her desire to be around him. "Mischel that sounds like Mee-shell, not Michelle, how are you this morning, ma'am?"

"Oh, you're with him. The one you ignored me for at your book signing. Thank you, brother."

Laughing, Dr. Freeman responds, "Come on sister, it was not his fault. He is a very smart young man."

"I bet." Mischel does not offer Robert a hug. She reaches to shake Robert's hand. He is not offended and shakes her hand.

Dr. Freeman says, "Wow, I never noticed that."

"You never noticed what?" Mischel, assuming that he is saying something about her, asked.

"Where you were sitting. If you would have been directly in the center and looked out into the lake, you would be in between two rock formations that make the area look like a half-moon, Bengal tiger teeth, or bull horns. And if you turn to the west, you are directly between the two apartment buildings, and to the south is two large buildings with a pyramid in the center. This looks like an entrance point, a portal, or a vortex."

Mischel questions, "entrance point to what?"

Dr. Freeman asks Mischel, "do you want to walk with us? I'm going to give him some lessons. From the lessons, you may understand what I mean by entrance point."

"Oh, women are allowed on this trip?"

"If you keep your attitude, you should stay here. The water is beautiful. It may calm your nerves."

"I'm sorry. I would love to join the two of you."

They walk closer to the water.

"Mischel, you should take some notes like Brother Robert."

Mischel takes a notepad and pen out of her bag.

The water current is strong. The waves are unusually flowing. Dr. Freeman starts with, "people are usually drawn to big bodies of water because it is a physical replication of the unseen energy grid. Everything is energy. Let's walk over there."

They walk to a section with cement pillars and a circle with a flagpole in the middle.

Dr. Freeman, unstartled, notices a car sitting with two white men taking pictures of them. He ignores them, pointing to the layout, he continues to talk to Robert and Mischel. "As we enter, we see four pillars around four feet tall, two on each side, separated by a sidewalk. Then we see seven pillars, three on the right side and four on the left side, seven pillars in all. Someone could be leaving a message, attempting to catch the right person's attention, informing them that the stability is in the seven liberal arts and sciences."

Robert touches each one on the left side like they will give him some magical powers.

Mischel looks at Robert like he has lost his mind. Her face forms to say, "what are you doing dummy?"

Dr. Freeman continues, "let me further explain. As we walk down the sidewalk, we see 4 pillars on the left side and 3 on the right side. The number 4 means stability or organization. It also indicates the 4 elements, air, water, fire, and earth. 3 represents creativity. In total there are 7. The number 7 means the mysteries. It can also indicate a mystic, preacher, or teacher."

Robert touches the pillars on the right side. And again, Mischel looks at him like he is lost his mind.

"The 7 plus the 4 pillars equal 11. In numerology, the number 11 represents a master inspirer or an inspiring lesson to be mastered. It also indicates that an initiate has been found worthy to earn higher knowledge."

Mischel jokingly asks, "have we been found worthy?"

"I do not know, have you?" Dr. Freeman seriously looks at Mischel. He points to the circle. "Here we have two pillars. If you look closely it looks like the number 11. Let's walk through the pillars."

"Can't a circle represent spirituality? I read somewhere that this is what it means," Mischel asks.

Nodding his head, Dr. Freeman answers, "Yes, in several mystical orders that is exactly what it means."

Mischel seems proud that she knew the answer.

"Robert, would you like to count how many cube structures are on top?"

Robert, saying nothing starts counting. He touches each one. "There are 14."

Dr. Freeman explains, "the number 14 means many things. If we use the Ancient Egyptian technique of "As Above, So Below," the number 14 means a person who is stable with self.

In the Christian mysteries, 14 represents the foundation of Christ."

"WOW! You are saying that Christianity has a deeper meaning? Now that is new," Robert expresses.

"Mischel would you like to count the little poles."

"Sure. I won't be touching them though." She looks at Robert like he just finished digging in his nose. "There are 15 gates with 10 poles each. Easy math, 15 times 10 is 150."

"Anytime we see a zero at the end of a number, we know it represents the divinity of God. So, 150 is 15 and 0. In this case, the number 15 is touched by God."

"What does the number 15 mean, Dr. Freeman?" Mischel inquires.

"I'll explain in a few minutes.

In the center, we see a circle with a pole. The American flag is on it.

I need you to pay attention now. One day you may need to remember how I see things." Dr. Freeman wipes the sweat off his forehead. "The flagpole coming out the center of the circle is the birthing process.

The 14 pillars and the flagpole equal 15. The 15th letter in the alphabet is O, which is a 360-degree circle. The number 15 means Christ Consciousness. In this case, the structure indicates, the divine consciousness of Christ is born. The idea of Christ is crucial in understanding the individual self. When totaling the letters, in Christ together, we get the number 32. 32 represents power. Other words that equal 32 are circle, power, glory, and America.

Going back to the 150, when the number 0 is behind a number, it means God's divine power. So, 150 means God's divine power with Christ Consciousness. The American Flag representative the divine power of Christ's Conscious.

Do you have all that?"

"Yes," Mischel and Robert simultaneously respond.

"Let's walk out of the circle. We know who walked in, but do we know who is walking out." Dr. Freeman looks at the two of them. They both look as if what he said went over their heads. "If a picture were taken of this structure from a plane, it would look like a European ankh. On to the next structure."

Robert asks, "don't you mean an Egyptian ankh?" Robert never heard or saw a European ankh before.

"No, a European one."

They walk in silence. Dr. Freeman is sharing so much information that Mischel and Robert look a little overwhelmed. He aggressively pushes forward as if he does not care like a man on a mission. It could be because of his age or the alignment of the day and time. As they leave the second site, Dr. Freeman looks at the car with the white men, wanting them to know that he sees them. He points at the structure.

When they arrive, Dr. Freeman pauses before he starts speaking. "Looking up the hill across the street, we see three mansions. We are at the 3rd site. When we turn around to face the water, there are 5 pillars on our right side. The sidewalk separates them from 7 more pillars. It is the 3, 5, 7 of the Masons. 3+5+7= 15.

From a different angle, there are 4 pillars on the right. Then there are 3 pillars in a half-circle forming a hook, like a letter J or an Egyptian crook. This is 3, 4, 5. The numbers used for the Pythagorean Triangle.

The sidewalk lays out in a pattern around this patch of grass. Robert, go to that corner."

Robert walks to the corner.

Dr. Freeman than instructs, "Mischel go stand on the circle at that corner."

She walks and stands on the circle.

Dr. Freeman yells, "Remember how we are standing." He waves for them to come back to him.

They quickly walk back.

"There's no coincidence that it is in a Pythagorean Triangle shape. The numbers associated with the triangle are 3, 4, and 5.

Milwaukee is known to be a place of occultism. One way of recognizing this is by the number of Gargoyles throughout the city. Gargoyles are like evil angels or cherubim who built and protected Solomon's Temple."

The car with the men watching them pulls off.

CHAPTER 9

After Dr. Freeman shows them the sights, he decides to exercise and walks back to where they first saw Mischel. Robert and Mischel, who are now his students, follow him. He begins an exercise that looks as graceful as Tai Chi as Mischel watches, moving her body, imitating his moves.

Robert, on the other hand, sits on a bench, looking at his notes and staring off into the distance. Several minutes pass, Robert suddenly blurts out, "Dr. Freeman, I have a question."

"OK," Dr. Freeman continues to exercise.

"Why does it seem like you focus a lot on what white people did?"

Dr. Freeman stops, "explain…"

"You talk about the bible a lot. You even brought up the GREEK PHILOSOPHER PYTHAGORAS."

Mischel chimes in, "I was thinking the same thing."

"Where did the Greek philosophers get their information?"

"From the Africans, why not just teach what the Africans taught them?" Robert asks.

"Robert, remember everything is a process. There are steps.

When we realize Europeans were students, often great students of Africans, we should understand they received at least the first degrees. Greek philosophers like Pythagoras and Aristotle, who some claim were black men, recorded the degrees. Next, their students and they deconstructed the information to get a better understanding. Then they reconstructed relevant information to explain it more logically for their way of life."

"I do not understand," Mischel adds.

"In other words, if Africans taught certain Europeans, this means they have the basic information. How many of us can honestly say we have the basic information taught by Ancient Africans?"

Robert replies, "not many."

"Exactly. The European students'
books, especially the Bible, are the
opening to the vortex into the African
mind. The African mind is the closest
mind to the creating force."

Robert asks another question, "but
why do you think the Bible is so
important?"

"Many books written after 1611 A.D.
have been heavily influenced by the
Bible."

Mischel asks, "influenced? I know
the book was used to enslave us." She
says the same thing as Robert said.
Robert nods his head in agreement.

"True, the interpretations of the
universal laws within the Bible
enslaved many. The universal laws are
so powerful they were used for good or
bad. The verse in the Bible which
states, "God has no favorites," is
proof that the law is the law,"
explains Dr. Freeman.

"That book is filled with man-made
law," Robert interrupts.

"This is true, as well. However, the
book must be thoroughly studied to get
a better understanding of how Europeans
interpret human behavior. The Bible is

also the spiritual guide for America, not in the religious sense, but in the sense of how energy flows within the universal order of things. The written energy patterns are in folklore and mythology. If you study the Bible, you will understand the European mentality."

Robert confusingly says, "I don't know, but I'll give it a thought."

"You have a gift, Robert. Close your eyes and think about Africans teaching Europeans about universal laws to get them out of their savage state."

Robert closes his eyes. He imagines an African wearing a white jalabiya and a small red fez teaching Greeks wearing togas. The African teacher is holding the writings of Tehuti. He points at a line.

The Greeks are students intensely looking in awe as if to say, how can this one book teach the sciences of the universe. He never imagined anything like this before. It's like something secretly implanted into his brain.

"Do not be so hard on European writings that you miss the African lesson. You and Mischel go to an empty page."

Robert opens his eyes. They both have an empty page.

Dr. Freeman continues, "Turn the page sideways. You may need some room to write."

They follow his instructions.

"Now make 9 columns. On top, number the columns 1 through 9. Put "A" in the first column. The letter "B" in the second column. The letter "I" should go in the 9th column." Dr. Freeman looks at what they wrote. He satisfied, so he continues, "the letter "J" is the 10th letter, but 1+0=1. So, with "J" put it in the first column. Go all the way until you get to the letter "Z" which should be in the 8th column."

1	2	3	4	5	6	7	8	9
A	B	C	D	E	F	G	H	I
J	K	L	M	N	O	P	Q	R
S	T	U	V	W	X	Y	Z	

Mischel asks, "is this the numerology chart?"

"Yes, this is the Pythagoras system. But it comes from the Ahmose Papyrus. The difference is the hieroglyphics.

There are also different forms of numerology, but I'll stick with this one."

"Hieroglyphic, these letters and numbers aren't Egyptian," Robert rebuttals.

"I'm glad you recognize this, Robert. The letters are shapes just like the Egyptian hieroglyphics are shapes. The numbers are shapes used in the Arabic language."

Robert, once again, looks doubtful.

"Stop looking like Africans didn't give this system to Europeans," Dr. Freeman chastises Robert.

"Yeah Robert," Mischel teases.

"Are you ready for your first numerology lesson?"

Mischel and Robert both say, "Yes."

"Ok, let's use the word, Genesis. It is spelled G-E-N-E-S-I-S."

They write it down, seemingly competing against each other while looking at the chart. Then write the number equivalent to the letter. G is

7, E is 5, N is 5, E is 5, S is 1, I is 9, and S is 1.

Mischel finishes first. "I got 33."

"I did something wrong. I got 32."

"You're right, Robert, you did something wrong. If you don't add the numbers right using this system, you will misinterpret the entire thing. This reason is why you must be cautious."

While Dr. Freeman was talking, Robert adds the numbers up again. "Ok, I got 33 this time."

"Good, both of you did well. Usually, we would reduce the numbers. In other words, we would add each number together. In this case, we have the number 33 or double 3s. We will leave it as 33. We call this a master number."

Mischel inquires, "do we leave it even when we have other numbers to add to it?"

"That is a good question. The answer is NO."

Both Mischel and Robert are
interested in this. It is like solving
a puzzle.

"Each number has several meanings.
All depending on where it is placed.
Two of the meanings of the master
number 33 is a master teacher or master
lesson."

"Why is it a master number? Aren't
all numbers master numbers?"

"All numbers can be mastered but are
not master numbers. Numbers vibrate on
different frequencies. In the early
days, the master numbers were 11, 22,
and 33. As time went on, they added the
numbers 44, 55, 66, 77, 88, and 99.

With the word Genesis, it adds to
33. To reduce it, we add 3+3, which
equals 6. It would look like the number
33 with a slash and the number 6
(33/6).

The number 6 is the base number.
Therefore, the energy of the word
Genesis changes between the 33rd and
6th vibrations. The word or person, if
this is a person's name, will vibrate
either on a master level or base level.
The intensity is much higher on the
master level. It is so powerful that

nothing can live under the vibration continuously.

The base number allows the thing or person to rest before attempting to vibrate on a master level. Master numbers have a great demand and return a great reward."

"Numbers have that much power?" Mischel inquires.

"Oh yes, it is the first science out of 4 that were taught to the Europeans by the Africans. We call it numerology today. It was arithmetic before."

Mischel asks, "What are the other sciences?"

"Geometry, music, and astronomy."

"Is astronomy what we call astrology today?" Mischel asks again.

"You got it, similar to the difference between esoteric and exoteric information," Dr. Freeman smiles. He is happy she caught on. "This is how we can read a person. If we calculate their birth date and full name, we can pretty well predict their actions and where to guide them."

"Is this why you asked if I had a middle name?" Robert questions.

"Yeah, Dr. Freeman, is this why?"

"Exactly why."

Robert further probes, "can this system be done throughout the bible?"

Dr. Freeman smiles even harder, "yes, yes, it can, but it has to be within the occult written King James Version, hidden words, meanings, or messages exist in the text. However, it doesn't mean that every word or Bible verse has a special meaning. Robert, do you know the name for bible interpretation?"

"No sir."

"Hermeneutics"

"How do you spell that Dr. Freeman?"

"H-E-R-M-E-N-E-U-T-I-C-S"

Robert writes the word down. "Dr. Freeman, it has the same beginning as Hermaphrodite. So, this has something to do with Hermes too?" Robert excitingly responds.

Mischel looks frustrated, having no clue what they are talking about, "Hello."

"Don't worry Mischel, you'll catch up one day," Robert teases her in return.

"Okay smart guy," Mischel sarcastically responds. She questions Dr. Freeman, "You said this system could tell us a lot about people if I heard you correctly?"

"You heard me correctly. It can tell us what a person is to learn in this lifetime. It can tell us who the person is. It also can tell us how other people see the person or interpret the person's vibration. It can also explain the person's destiny."

"It can tell us all that?" Mischel is surprised.

"It can tell us much more, but that is enough for now, a little homework for you. Do your names. I'll email you some meanings based on the numbers. I will share one more thing with you then I have to leave for a meeting. Robert, go back to your notes from earlier."

Robert flips back in his notebook.

"Go to the part about Genesis 1:1 through Genesis 2:2."

Robert replies, "there were 33 verses in between, I remember."

"Mischel look with Robert at his notes."

Mischel moves close to Robert. She is shocked.

Robert states, "I'm not wearing Egyptian Musk."

"Obviously," Mischel snaps back.

Dr. Freeman responds, "alright youngsters."

They laugh and focus on Robert's notes.

"Robert, I'm glad you remembered how many verses there were. Now take the colons from between 1:1 and 2:2. What do you see?"

Robert does not quite understand, but Mischel does. "I see the numbers 11 and 22."

Robert says, "oh I get it. Here are the master numbers 11, 22, and 33."

Dr. Freeman nods his head in approval, "One more thing, the number 33 means what?"

Robert starts flipping the pages to find the answer.

Mischel quickly replies, "master teacher or master lesson."

Dr. Freeman says in a loud voice, "exactly, Robert what did we point out in Genesis 2:2?"

Robert flips the pages back again. He forgot to write this part down. "Ah, Dr. Freeman, I forgot to write it down."

"In the verse, it spoke about the 7th day of creation."

"Now I remember, they are the 7 laws taught by Hermes."

"And that is the master lesson. I must go now. I'm late."

"Thank you for your time, Dr. Freeman," Mischel gratefully responds.

"Dr. Freeman, I don't want to hold you up. I can make it back home from here. You've helped me enough today. Thank you."

"Both of you are welcome. Enjoy the rest of your day."

The real reason Robert didn't ride back with Dr. Freeman is that he remembers lessons from Cue. Once, Robert questioned why so many people drowned in that part of the lake. Cue thought someone was doing a ritual, and drownings were sacrifices.

Now, Robert thinks about the pyramids that Dr. Freeman pointed out. In front of the pyramids in Egypt sits a sphinx. Robert wonders if the cement structure located on a different part of the lakefront could represent the sphinx. So, he walks to the area and stands on the bridge, looking at the small sidewalk leading to a large circle with an arch, like the one at the doorway that Dr. Freeman showed. Robert walks down from the bridge to stand in the middle of it and looks at the pyramids. Then he turns around to face the other structures they are somewhat aligned. He says a prayer to unlock the secret of the sphinx.

Then he walks back to the doorway, standing at it, he counts the bricks on the ground. There are 12 in all. He walks to the center of the structure and counts the lines. From each side, the centerline is the seventh, standing on the line, he stares into the water, wondering if something was coming in or leaving out. He turns around and realizes that he is directly between two buildings far off in the distance. It was like he was standing between 2 pillars, reminding him of the Africology House.

He decides to find the buildings, but first, he walks past the other sights, saying a prayer at each one. Eventually he locates the proper buildings less than a mile away. The first one is on E. Lafayette Place. He sees a wall connecting the buildings, curiously wanting to know about the builder, knowing the builder must be a master.

Then he walks to the intersection of E. Lafayette Place and N. Prospect Avenue, continuing to walk along the brick wall until the end of the second building, and turns around to go and stand in between the buildings. On the way back, he looks at the sidewalk on his right side, which has cross shapes. He read somewhere that cross shapes represent faces or elements, and an "x" shape represents points or fire. He turns back to the building. The number in the center of the building is 2020.

Little does he know 2020 hides the master number 22 or the master builder. When the number is hidden, it has a different meaning. Now, the number 22 means the secret magician. He writes in his notebook the address 2020 N. Prospect Avenue, wondering what the word prospect means. One of the meanings is vision. He automatically thinks of 20/20 vision. Could this be a sign of something important happening in 2020? He would ask Dr. Freeman.

CHAPTER 10

For two weeks, several groups target different parts of Milwaukee's inner city. It looks like an all-out war. Protesters are mostly peaceful except for the few who are targeting businesses. They break into stores as others loot the stores.

Police mobilize their command vehicle. They are monitoring the cameras strategically placed throughout the city. While other law enforcement officers from different departments around the state dress in military-style riot gear with high-powered rifles patrol the streets.

Later that evening, there's a loud bang. Cue's door is violently kicked open. Several police officers rush in wearing full riot gear. Cue's mates, including Diamond, scream in horror.

An Officer demands, "Where is he at?"

Ebony responds, "Who?"

"Do not be a stupid little girl."

She is upset that the officer called her a little girl. She sarcastically replies, "Who are you talking about?"

"CHARLES UMAR EDWARDS"

"Who is that?"

"Okay, you want to play dumb. Where is Cue? Does that stupid name ring a bell."

Jazmine concerned. looks at her co-wife, "He is not here."

The 2nd officer responds, "We've been surveilling the house all day. We saw the bastard come in, but we didn't see him leave. We know he is here.

Nefer asks, "Do you have a search warrant?"

An officer slaps her as if he were trying to break her jaw.

She is shocked. She starts crying as she grabs her face. Blood is leaking from her lip and nose.

The 1st officer arrogantly says, "Ouch, that slap should let you know that we aren't playing games with you."

The 3rd officer orders, "Men, go look for the black rat. And bring him here."

The remaining officers follow the instructions. They begin tearing up the house. Several minutes later, they return with Cue.

A black officer announces, "The black coward was hiding under the bed. While his women were out here protecting him. He's no different. He is just like those pimps and hustlers who use women for their wants, COWARD."

Cue sarcastically replies, "Do I hear a little jealousy in your voice?"

The black officer hits Cue in the head with the bud of his rifle.

Cue's head swells as blood gushes out.

"Does it sound like I'm playing with you, boy?"

"You seem like a coon to me, sell-out. How much are they paying you?"

The black officer aims his rifle at Cue's face to shoot him.

The 3rd officer who seems to be in charge jumps in, "Hold on, that is not why we're here. I'm sure you will get your pleasure if he doesn't give us the information we want. Call him in."

Cue is handcuffed and tied to a chair. His mates stare in horror as they hug each other.

Another officer calmly states, "Everything is clear. You can come in."

George Gardner enters wearing a dark blue suit and red tie. He flashes a police badge. "So, you're the famous leader of these streets that we've heard so much about."

Cue sits silently with pride that the man recognizes his power. He has no clue who the man is, so he knows he has to be cautious.

"I'm DETECTIVE Gardner with MILWAUKEE POLICE DEPARTMENT SPECIAL TASK FORCE."

Cue shrugs his shoulders, not caring about George.

"Do you know these men?" He shows a picture of Dr. Freeman and Robert together speaking.

Cue does not say a word.

"You can be stubborn, but we have intel that they are planning to harm you."

Cue is now frustrated, "RT isn't going to do nothing. He does not have the heart."

"So, you do know these men?"

"Yeah, I am aware of them."

George points to Robert. "So, this is one of your loyal generals."

"He means nothing to me. All I know him as is a traitor."

"A traitor? You shouldn't have any problem giving up info about him then. What information has Dr. Freeman shared with your general?"

"I told you he is nothing to me. He is a deserter. He is not the general type."

"I'm not concerned about your lover quarrel. I'll ask you one more time before I let these officers take their manly frustration out on your little ladies."

The 2nd officer says, "I would love to take my manhood out on them. They look like fun."

"They can be replaced. Do what you have to do."

George nods at an officer. Several of them take Cue's mates to the back. The women scream as one yells in agony.

"OK, OK!!! Hold on, I don't know what the doctor has told him. I haven't talked to RT since he left my house."

George harshly replies, "Glad you came to your senses. Now get rid of your childish pride and find out what your general knows. Or the next time we return, we will finish you and your love triangle. Get it?"

Cue nods in affirmative.

"Good, I'll see you in a few days. Let the bastard go."

Two officers free Cue. Then they leave.

Cue's mates, except for Nefer, rush into the room, hugging and kissing him. Nefer, cut by an officer, slowly strolls in as she holds her bloody hand over her neck. Cue looks and sees it is only a flesh wound. He pushes them away, quickly finding one of his burner phones to contact his generals. He does not know if the police have uncovered that they are maneuvering the people during the unrest.

Cue does not stop the entire operation, instructing his generals to beef up the political agenda. His idea remains that out of chaos comes order, having their hands in the order, he wants to establish himself as the go-to man when ideas are tossed around about the black community. He hates that people can come into the neighborhood and work on the roads, inconveniencing the residents at will.

Cue once said that he had no problem if a rumor starts about him being responsible for the uprising, if it cannot be proven. It shows that he is an intellect who wields power. The only person who was in the room during the initial planning phase was Robert. He must contact Robert in a way that makes him look like he made a mistake. The question is, will Robert accept it?

CHAPTER 11

Robert is in his living room, sitting at his computer desk, looking at the notes he wrote. At the same time, he is researching information on his computer. Books are scattered all over the floor.

With a look of disgust, as if in pain, Robert looks through the bible. Although he is still very doubtful of its good nature, he took the time to add all the book names in the New Testament.

- Matthew (4.1.2.2.8.5.5=27)
- Mark (4.1.9.2=16)
- Luke (3.3.2.5=13)
- John (1.6.8.5=20)
- Acts (1.3.2.1=7)
- Romans (9.6.4.1.5.1=26)
- 1 Corinthians (3.6.9.9.5.2.8.9.1.5.1=58+1=59)
- 2 Corinthians (3.6.9.9.5.2.8.9.1.5.1=58+2=60)
- Galatians (7.1.3.1.2.9.1.5.1=30)
- Ephesians (5.7.8.5.1.9.1.5.1=42)
- Philippians (7.8.9.3.9.7.7.9.1.5.1=66)
- Colossians (3.6.3.6.1.1.9.1.5.1=36)
- 1 Thessalonians (2.8.5.1.1.1.3.6.5.9.1.5.1=48+1=49)

- 2 Thessalonians
(2.8.5.1.1.1.3.6.5.9.1.5.1=48+2=50)
  - 1 Timothy (2.9.4.6.2.8.7=38+1=39)
  - 2 Timothy (2.9.4.6.2.8.7=38+2=40)
  - Titus (2.9.2.3.1=17)
  - Philemon (7.8.9.3.5.4.6.5=47)
  - Hebrews (8.5.2.9.5.5.1=35)
  - James (1.1.4.5.1=12)
  - 1 Peter (7.5.2.5.9=28+1=29)
  - 2 Peter (7.5.2.5.9=28+2=30)
  - 1 John (1.6.8.5=20+1=21)
  - 2 John (1.6.8.5=20+2=22)
  - 3 John (1.6.8.5=20+3=23)
  - Jude (1.3.4.5=13)
  - Revelation (9.5.4.5.3.1.2.9.6.5=49)

Robert takes the paper he writes the calculations on and tacks it to the wall, placing it next to a paper with the alphabet's numerology equivalence. Another piece of paper shows a layout of the Pythagoras triangle. It has boxes attached to every line of the triangle. Inside the boxes are people. The smallest triangle has a man with equation 3x3 under him. The middle triangle has a woman with the equation 4X4 under her. The largest triangle has a child with the equation 5X5 under the child.

There is a whiteboard on the wall with notes scribbled on it. There is also a picture of Diamond hanging up. He also has a certificate he received

for his membership in Cue's
organization.

He becomes curious about the word
Milwaukee. So, he adds it up.

- M-4
- i-9
- l-3
- w-5
- a-1
- u-3
- k-2
- e-5
- e-5

The word Milwaukee equals 37,
reduced it equals 10, and 10 reduced
equals 1. The number 1 is the first
masculine number, which means an
individual is a stubborn person or has
a too giving personality. The person
can be an executive working best alone.
In the case of Milwaukee, the city is
masculine.

However, Robert is curious about the
number 37. He separates the 3 and 7,
wondering if it could have a combined
meaning sort of like the Egyptian
teaching "As above; so below." The
number 3 represents creativity in
things like acting, journalism,
writing, and lecturing. Again, the
number 7 represents the mysteries

taught by a mystic, a teacher, or a preacher who understands the mind sciences, which can transform a person, place, or thing into an enigma.

Robert puts the two numbers together and writes, "Milwaukee is a place of mystical endeavors and creations." He does not know if the statement is true but vows to find out.

He doses off tired from all the studying he has been doing. Suddenly, something crashes through his window. Glass flies everywhere, followed by bullets as plaster falls from the walls and ceiling. He has no clue where the shots are coming. The only thing he can do is get on the floor and low crawl like an Army soldier to the back of his couch.

The shots ring out for about a minute, but to Robert, it seems like hours. A car screeches off at a high rate of speed. He doesn't move, lying on the floor, he listens closely, not knowing if the shooter is in the car that left. After several minutes he slowly crawls to the light switch to turn it off. Then he makes his way to the shattered window, being careful not to touch any broken glass, looking out, he does not see anyone.

He then looks for what came through the window, a brick, slowly he opens a paper tied to it with a rope that reads, "TRAITOR."

He finds his phone to make a call.

"Hello," the person sounds as if he is waking up from a deep sleep.

Robert stays quiet for a second.

Obviously agitated, the person repeats, "HELLO!"

Robert finally but nervously says, "Dr. Freeman, someone just shot up my house."

"Are you all right?"

"Yes, just shaken up."

"I need you to stay there. I'm going to make some arrangements for you. I'll call you right back." Dr. Freeman hangs up the phone.

Robert remains on the floor. Several minutes go by, before the phone rings. Without looking at the phone, he answers it. "Dr. Freeman."

"You're still dealing with that charlatan?"

"Oh, what's up Cue?"

"Just checking on my top general. How are you?"

Robert suspiciously replies, "this is not a good time to talk. I'll call you back in a few." He is more suspicious and begins thinking Cue called a hit. Robert knows Cue has the type of power.

"Call me back when you get some time. I was kinda harsh. We need to catch up."

Robert is convinced that Cue set him up. "OK," he hangs up the phone. The phone rings again. He looks at it this time. It is Dr. Freeman. "Doc, Cue just called me. I think he had his people do this."

"We'll figure all that out later. I'm sending a driver over there now. He'll honk 3 times pause and honk 1 more time. You'll know it is my guy. He'll bring you to my location."

"OK, Doc, thank you." Robert packs, not knowing what to expect from Dr. Freeman, but he knew he couldn't stay at his house for the night.

A car arrives approximately 15 minutes later. The driver honks three times and then once. Robert looks out the window of his dark house to find the location of the car, hoping someone is not waiting for him in the shadows. He decides to make a run for the car, jumps up, and runs out. Around the same time, the police begin to arrive.

Eventually, the car pulls up to Dr. Freeman's location. The only light is coming from the stars. Robert nervously looks up into the sky. There seem to be shooting stars, but something is not right as a few of them change colors zig-zagging back and forth.

The car stops. He nervously shakes off what he saw. He looks around before getting out, not seeing much, or recognizing the part of the city that the car drove.

"Over here, Robert," Dr. Freeman instructs as he flashes a light.

Robert cautiously walks towards Dr. Freeman. He is a total wreck.

"We do not need to talk. I want you to get in that car over there." Dr. Freeman points to a different car than the one that just dropped him off. "I have a private plane waiting for you."

"Wait…"

"Either you trust me, or your life may be in danger. Thank me later. I'll see you in a few days."

Robert nods his head as he shakes Dr. Freeman's hand, ducking and looking around, he heads towards the car and gets in. The car drives off.

CHAPTER 12

A few hours later, Robert gets off a plane and walks to a car. It drives off at a high rate of speed. Robert is stunned. Eventually, he sees an 80 MPH speed limit sign. Another sign reads Mexico 20 miles. The driver is heading towards the Mexican border.

The border guard waves them through without being checked when they get there. It seems very odd to Robert. The whole trip, he has not said a word.

The car stops. Robert gets out as an unknown man greets him. The man is wearing all black with a symbol on his shirt.

"Welcome, Robert."

"Thank you, sir," Robert does not think to ask the man his name. He is just going with the flow, trusting Dr. Freeman has his best interest.

"I am detailed to take care of you and your needs while you're here."

"Dr. Freeman has connections like that? Wow."

"You will learn more as time passes. I know you're tired. So, let's go to your hotel.

Here are a cell phone and my number. When you get up, call me. We'll make further arrangements." The man drives Robert to the hotel. He hands him a key with a room number on it.

Robert exits the car, taking a deep breath as he looks around at the scenery, feeling a great sense of relief not worrying about anyone getting him here. It is Mexico, he thinks. He never had a desire to be in Mexico.

He always wanted to go to Africa because Cue spoke of how beautiful it was and the many opportunities there. Cue often painted a picture with his words of starting a community in Africa. He presented the idea that black people in America had all the skills needed to develop, cultivate, and govern an area.

He would talk about the pyramids. Then all The Family would discuss how they thought the Egyptians lived. One thought was that the pyramids were healing centers because their shape harnessed energies.

Another thought was they were UFOs embedded in the earth, lying dormant until it was time to reignite. Still, another was they were built as a calendar to tell the correct day and time, helping the farmers prepare for the yearly floods and planting cycle. All in all, they had no definite answer to what they were. Yet, they enjoyed creatively speaking about their purpose.

CHAPTER 13

Dr. Freeman enters Jacob's office, walking to his favorite chair, he sits down. Jacob is already seated across from him. Dr. Freeman gets out of his chair, noticing a new picture hanging on the wall and walks over to look at it. After examining it, he returns to the chair to sit down.

"Doc, what have you been doing lately? Any new discoveries?"

"Nothing new uncovered, just have a question for you."

"By all means old friend, ask away."

"What's going on with Cue and you?"

"What do you mean?"

"Something horrible happened to Robert last shadow. He thinks Cue and his ruthless gang tried to kill him."

"I don't know anything about that. I've only advised Cue on important elements in the city. You know, the ones which could cripple its very fabric."

"But why, why would you tell him those things? He is young and radical. He could get himself into big trouble."

"He is a lot more intelligent and patient than you think. Don't let your insecurities confuse you. He is a natural-born leader. I saw it the first time we met him. He is a combination of all the leaders in our brotherhood."

Dr. Freeman sinks into his chair. He cannot believe Jacob's words.

Jacob emphatically states, "In fact, he has built a powerful organization, since our brotherhood, in this city. With proper guidance from us, he could do the miracle that we've failed to do.

He has an influence over enough young people to where they can truly disrupt the city's entire political machine. With numbers like he has, it could be a great benefit to us as well."

Dr. Freeman cautions, "That may be more dangerous than you want to admit, especially if he is responsible for what happened to Robert last night."

"You never explained what happened?"

"Someone shot up his house, nearly killing him."

"Oh no, and you think it was Cue."

"From what I know, at this time, Cue and his people are the only ones who would want to harm him."

"Why do you think that? Aren't they all in the same group?"

Dr. Freeman looks suspicious. If Jacob has spoken to Cue, he would think that Cue told him Robert is no longer involved with Cue's family. "You haven't heard?"

"Heard what?"

"Robert is no longer a part of them."

"No, I didn't know that. Is Robert alright?"

Dr. Freeman does not believe that Jacob is unaware. It shows in his face. "Yes, he survived the shooting without any physical injury, I can't say the same for his mental state."

"Is there anything that we can do for the young man?"

"I already got him out of the city."

Jacob looks disturbed like his plan has been interrupted by Dr. Freeman's move. "Well, at least he is alright." Jacob gets out of his seat. He walks to the coffee maker to pour himself a cup of coffee. "Would you like a cup, Doc?"

"Sure."

"Cream and sugar?"

"Both, thank you."

Jacob carefully prepares their cups of coffee, carrying Dr. Freeman's to him, and handing him the cup, then returns to his seat. He sits down like he is relieved. "I hope it is good. I take pride in what I make."

"I'm sure it will be fine. You've always had a talent for making drinks."

Jacob sips his coffee. Then leans his head back into the chair. "Remember the old days when our craft seems like an unbreakable brotherhood. Those days seem long gone. This new generation seems to not want anything to do with us."

Dr. Freeman nods his head.

"I miss those days when the brotherhood was feared but honored."

"Mostly an honor among thieves from what I remember. I remember the things done to get ahead. The murders, the threats, the destruction, pimping women, selling drugs, what's the honor in that?"

"But we took care of each other first. We controlled our communities."

Dr. Freeman senses are alerted. He sits up in his chair. What did Jacob mean? "Yes, we did to the detriment of others. Was it worth it?"

"Look at where we stand, I think it was all worth it."

"But the craft lost hundreds of members, since then. Some to death, others to disinterest."

"I believe people didn't lose interest because of our acts back in the days. I believe they lost interest because we became too competitive against each other, instead of bringing the best brothers into our order, we started accepting any caliber of man who supported each brother's personal agenda."

"Shouldn't everyone have a chance to learn?"

"Learning is one thing. Receiving our precious secrets to success is another thing."

"Speaking of secrets, what's up with George Gardner?"

"George is all talk. He is nothing. He just tries to intimidate people with his tough talk. He is harmless as a roach."

"I hope you're right. The Aaronites have lost a lot of power over the years. Remember what it was like when they held all the power. If they get a hold of the scrolls, things won't be good."

"I just contacted him for his money connection. We needed it for you to complete your work in Mexico. If you retrieve the scroll, we will have a much better world."

"One thing you're right about is he has big money. But sometimes big money is not good money. If the scrolls are retrieved, we then have to worry about protecting them, since the Aaronites have been informed."

Jacob smiles, "well this time it is good money. It will get us what we want."

"Let me get outta here. I have to go get my last affairs in order before I head out in the morning."

"Good idea, I'll see you when you return with the prize."

"And you know it," acknowledges Dr. Freeman.

They both get up to give their farewells. Dr. Freeman collapses when they walk towards each other.

"Doc, Doc, are you alright?" Jacob shakes Dr. Freeman getting no response. He calls his assistant into the office. His assistant enters the room and looks at Dr. Freeman. She starts administering CPR. While Jacob frantically calls 911.

The paramedics arrive about 10 minutes later. They immediately take over CPR.

They are too late. Dr. Freeman is pronounced dead.

CHAPTER 14

When he got into the room, he fell
asleep from pure exhaustion. Robert
wakes up the next day, not knowing the
time, yet the morning has passed. He
lays there looking at the ceiling,
thinking about what happened.

He gets out of bed to look around
the hotel room. The bed is plush. It
has a white goose feather and down
comforter. There is a flat-screen T.V.,
a recliner leather chair, a dresser,
and a desk.

He walks into the large, beautiful
brown bathroom. He first examines the
sliding glass shower. The showerhead
with over 20 different speeds and knobs
is silver. There is a marble double-
sink. The toilet is all white.

He walks out of the bathroom and
sits on the edge of the bed, turning on
the TV with the remote control. As he
flips through the channels, he knows
that there will be no TV today because
all the programs are in Spanish. He
turns it off and walks out on the
balcony. A beautiful hot sunny day,
Robert looks down at the Mexican

designed pool. He stays outside for a few minutes.

He realizes he is hungry. He takes a shower. Then he leaves the room headed for the restaurant.

Robert enters the restaurant. It has a colonial atmosphere, music playing as a big screen T.V. shows chefs preparing the food. As he walks in, he sees someone who looks familiar. He walks over to the young lady. "Mischel?"

"Oh, hi Robert. What are you doing here?"

"Long story, but Dr. Freeman made arrangements for me to be here."

"LEM made arrangements for me too. He is supposed to be meeting me down here tomorrow."

"Lem?"

"Yeah, you know, Lemuel. Dr. Lemuel Freeman."

"I always called him Dr. Freeman. I didn't even think of his first name."

"Lem is supposed to be introducing me to a band who needs a lead singer."

"You sing?"

Mischel rolls her eyes at Robert.
She sneeringly counters, "Do you think
I would be here if I couldn't?"

Robert looks at her with a smirk as
if to say whatever.

"I also speak Spanish. Lem wants me
to accompany him to some meeting, so I
can interpret what's being said."

"Sounds serious."

"I guess. It is about that book he
was lecturing about. I think they found
it down here."

"Is that right?"

"Honestly, all I know is it is some
book," she changes the subject, "So,
are you going to tell me why you're
here? Or are you going to keep playing
the mystery man role?"

"I'll play the mystery man for now."

"Whatever, you may as well take a
seat. Since you're the only person I
know here, you may as well keep me
company."

"Thank you, what are you eating?"

"I ordered a rib eye taco. Are you planning to order something? Or are you just here to keep me company?"

Robert laughs, "Yeah, I'm starving. Feels like I haven't eaten in a month."

"What's funny?"

"You. Anyways, how long have you been singing?"

"For as long as I can remember. It is my first love, after God and my family of course. I've dreamed of being a big-time entertainer. Although, I haven't done much work lately."

"Why not?"

"Life sometimes takes precedent over dreams. I have bills to pay."

"Your bills can't be that much." Robert waves over the waiter. At the same time, he sees his escort entering. "There's the man I'm supposed to meet later on."

"That is AHKHAH. He is Dr. Freeman's assistant here in Mexico. He is been doing the footwork here in Mexico while Dr. Freeman has been lecturing."

Ahkhah quickly approaches them. He is out of breath. He is an average build brown complexion man. He has what looks to be some tribal markings on his face. His beard and mustache are connected. He wears dread lots. He wears slightly tinted glasses with a straight top frame. He is wearing a black t-shirt and black jeans. His clothes are wrinkled as if he just pulled them out of drawers and put them on. "Excuse me for the interruption, but I have a bit of bad news."

Robert and Mischel look worried. They do not know what to think.

Ahkhah announces, "The Honorable Dr. Lemuel Freeman has transitioned to be with the ancestors."

"What do you mean?" Mischel emotionally asks.

"He has passed away."

Mischel screams, "WHAT!!! It can't be true." She breaks down and starts crying. She is heartbroken.

Robert calmly asks, "What happened?"

Ahkhah replies, "I do not know exactly at this time. He was at the Illustrious Moletree's office when he collapsed. CPR was done on him. By the time the paramedics arrived, he had transitioned."

Mischel's crying becomes uncontrollable.

Robert gets out of his chair, walks over to her to console her. She buries her face into his stomach.

"Something does not sound right about that. Now what?" Robert is puzzled. He wonders if it has to do with what happened to him.

Ahkhah says, "I suggest we complete the mission he started."

"Which is?"

"Retrieve the sacred papyrus of Tehuti."

Robert responds with strength and confidence, "I think that is a good idea. I'm with it."

Ahkhah asks, "How about you Mischel?"

She nods her head in agreement. She is crying too hard to say a word.

"Excellent, I'll make the arrangements. Here's $1,000 US dollars' worth of Mexican Paso for each of you." He hands both Mischel and Robert the same amount of money.

"I'll contact you in a few days. For now, enjoy Mexico, the best you can under these horrific circumstances." Ahkhah leaves just as fast as he came.

Robert asks, "Mischel are you ok?"

"Does it look like it? I'm going to get my food to go. Then I'm going back to my room."

"Well, let me walk you to your room."

Mischel still is crying. Robert tells the waiter to pack up her food. When the waiter comes back with her food, she gets up without saying a word. She continues to sob and walks out of the restaurant. Robert follows.

The walk to their hotel seems like a hundred-mile hike. They didn't say a word to each other. Mischel looks like she is in deep thought. Her face is wet.

Robert looks around at the surroundings. He has always worked on paying attention to details of the environment he was in. At one point, Robert studied the Army Special Forces manual. He obsessively explored anything having Special Forces attached to its name. It could be a business book or a cookbook. He didn't care.

When they make it up to Mischel's room, she says, "Here we are Robert. Thank you for walking me up."

"I'm right next door if you need anything."

"I'll be alright. It is just a little hard to process. I just knew my prayers and dreams had been answered. He was such a gentleman."

"I'm sure you'll find another man like him. You are an incredibly beautiful, funny, and intelligent lady. Think about it, you chose a powerful man."

"What?"

"You chose Dr. Freeman. He is a highly intelligent and powerful man."

"Do you think I was interested in Dr. Freeman as a lover?"

"By the way, you were acting around him, yes."

Mischel immediately stops crying, "You're wrong. You must not know anything about Dr. Freeman?"

"Not really."

"Dr. Freeman is an expert in telling people about their future. He said I would find my true path here in Mexico and that he would introduce me to the people who would help me. Now that is not going to happen."

Robert shockingly responds, "It hasn't been the first time that I've been wrong."

"Plus, Dr. Freeman has several wives around the world. He practiced the ancient marriage traditions. I respect his wives and would never want to share my man."

"We're still in Mexico. Matter of fact, Ahkhah may know who Dr. Freeman was going to introduce you to. Don't give up hope just yet."

"You have a good point."

"Plus Dr. Freeman is now our guardian angel. He is like an ancestor to us. I know wherever he is, he is going to look out for us."

Mischel shivers as if she had a cold wind hit her. She looks around. "Did you feel that?"

"Feel what?"

"That cold breeze. Once you said that I felt something. It is as if he is here."

This time Robert is the one who looks at her like she lost her mind. It is too hot for a cold breeze. The wind isn't even blowing. He doubtingly replies, "You must have an intense connection to him. I didn't feel a thing."

"Well thank you, for walking me up here."

"My pleasure."

She gently closes the door. She didn't want Robert to leave, but she didn't want him to get any funny ideas, since he already believes she was trying to be romantically involved with Dr. Freeman. She was not upset with Robert's comment. Most of her life, people have commented that she comes off as if she is flirting.

Her thought quickly shifts back to Dr. Freeman's death. She confusingly paces the floor as her eyes tear up again. She begins to pack her suitcase, stops, then lays on her bed. A few seconds go by, and she gets out of bed, paces the floor again, gazing into her half-packed suitcase, she begins to cry again, frustratingly grabs her clothes, throwing them around the room. She sits down in front of the mirror, looking at herself, realizing that in such a short time of crying, she looks like a wreck.

Still crying, she stares in the mirror, placing her face in her hands. Then she lays her head on the desk. When she hears a whisper, which sounds like a male's voice. She looks around the room, thinking it is all in her mind.

"Mischel pronounced like Mee-shell, not Michelle," the whisper gets louder.

She knows the only person who has messed with her recently about her name is Dr. Freeman. But he has transitioned? She shakes her head, then looks in the mirror, and sees a reflection of Dr. Freeman.

She is startled and quickly jumps, looking behind her, no one is there.

She frantically looks around the room, still no one. The only one in the room, she nervously looks back into the mirror.

"It is me. You're not going crazy."

"But, but how?"

"All that will be answered throughout your journey. Do you remember when I told you to lift the veil of self-deceit?"

"I remember."

"Well, this is that time. Do not allow your frustration to turn into self-pity or self-contempt. Do not use this time as crutches for you to lean on, because you will cripple all that you've worked for."

"Yessir."

"Patience and time are sometimes better than strength and passion. Your dreams are true if you visualized correctly." Dr. Freeman's face fades away.

"Wait," she realizes he is gone. She sits in disbelief with the experience, knowing it happened but can only stare

into the mirror and wonder what other
strange things will occur on the trip.

CHAPTER 15

Robert enters his room, walks to the balcony, and opens the sliding door. It is too hot to stand outside. He slides the balcony door shut and looks out of the glass door off into the distance.

Eventually, he realizes he didn't get anything to eat, and he needs some clothes. He was in such a hurry that he left his packed bag at his house. He has not had a fresh pair of clothes in almost two days. He turns around, looking throughout the room, and notices a book on his bed. The book is called "The Distinguished Teachings of Thoth." He flips to a section which reads, now is the time to share the information. He closes the book and puts it down, contemplating the meaning.

He walks to the door. As he goes to grab the doorknob, he changes his mind. He decides to read more of the book. He starts to get sleepy and lays down for a moment, beginning to dose off, he changes his mind again and gets out of bed. He needs to get something to eat and purchase some clothes.

He leaves his room. As he passes by Mischel's room. He begins to knock on her door to see if she wants to go with him but decides to keep walking.

When he gets outside, he looks around again. There are vendors and stores all around the area. He starts walking, looking through windows like he is window shopping. As he walks, a well-dressed brown skin man with a khaki-colored short sleeve shirt and pants with shoes to match stops him. He wears a papyrus brimmed hat. He is wearing a facial hairstyle like Ahkhah.

The man says, "Hey young man, today the energy forces told me to give my possessions away. I have some clothes for you."

Robert looks at the man as if the man has lost his mind. It is a coincidence that they are about the same size. He doesn't realize that the man is Nathan, the banker from the Africology house.

"Well do you want to see them or not? I do not have all day."

Robert curiously asks, "can I see them first?"

"You think a well-dressed man like me would give you some rags? Man, let me show you. I ain't playin no games." Nathan opens his green military duffle bag and starts pulling his things out. He has a few pictures on top, one being Benjamin Franklin flying a kite.

Robert states, "that's odd."

"Hold up, I'm going to show you I ain't playin no games."

"I'm talking about the picture of Benjamin Franklin."

"Oh, you like that?"

"Wondering more why a black man has a framed picture of Franklin."

"This is a powerful picture. You must not know much about him?"

"I know he was a Statesman and one of the first millionaires in America."

"That is all you know."

"Yeah."

"Well let me school you, youngster." Nathan positions the picture so Robert can take a better look at it. "Look at it more closely."

Robert sarcastically says, "I see it. A white man flying a kite. Doesn't mean much to me."

"You do not see the symbolism of this picture?"

"NO."

"You haven't paid much attention to your initiation info I see."

"Initiation info?"

"Never mind, let me drop some jewels on you. By first asking you how he became a millionaire."

"He probably owned some slaves. I don't know."

"Typical thought of the less learnt."

Robert looks at Nathan as if he disrespected him.

"Could his wealth have something to do with the lightning hitting the kite?" Nathan asks.

"I do not recall him inventing anything using electricity."

"Exactly, meaning this picture means something else. A kite, a golden key, and lightning have no real connection in that day and time."

"Right."

"But it does if you are a member of a secret or sacred brotherhood."

"How? I've been a part of a brotherhood, a family as we call it."

"Patience and I'll tell you. The kite is flying high in the sky. The lightning hits it, causing electricity to travel down the string assumingly because of the key. Do you get it yet?"

"NO!"

"Wow. The kite flying high means a higher realm of knowledge. The lesson of the higher knowledge or the key to his wealth is electricity or energy."

"You got all that from this picture."

"I explained it to you, didn't I?"

"How will this help me?"

"You said you are a part of a brotherhood. I can only assume that you went through an initiation.

Benjamin Franklin also went through several initiations, most of them occurring in France. One being the Freemasons. Do you know the significance of France?"

Robert is surprised and curious. He responds, "not at all."

"This was a hub of higher learning taught to selected Europeans by Africans. Never allow skin complexion to stop you from receiving knowledge. Always remember that." The man stops talking and pulls all the clothes out of his duffle bag. He lays them out neatly.

Robert watches him, still letting the info about Benjamin Franklin absorb.

"What do you think?" Nathan asks.

"These are sharp. How much do you want for them?"

Laughing, Nathan says, "I'm giving them to you. You forgot what I said. The energy forces told me to give everything away and you looked like the perfect size to fit these clothes."

"Thank you, sir."

"My pleasure. Here, take the duffle bag, you might need this to carry them. You can't have the pictures though, you ain't ready for these types of jewels." Nathan picks up the pictures. He walks off without saying another word.

CHAPTER 16

Jacob makes a phone call. Cue, surrounded by his wives, one on each side of him and Diamond sitting on the floor between his legs, answers his phone, hangs up, then dials a number. Khufu picks up then dials Nasir's number. They speak for a moment, hanging up after a conversation.

Mischel and Robert receive a telegram from Ahkhah. Nine days have passed. Instructed not to bring anything, they are to meet Ahkhah in the hotel lobby in the morning.

The next morning, Mischel is already sitting in the lobby as Robert walks in. He is surprised to see Khufu and Nasir there. "NASIR?"

"RT, what's the odds of seeing you here?"

"I was just thinking the same thing."

Mischel walks over to them. "Good morning, Robert. Do you know them?"

"Yes, we are a part of the same family."

Khufu maliciously says, "used to be a part of the same family. See your friend, RT here, decided to kick the family to the curb scared to make a black power move."

"Is that true, Robert?"

Robert upsettingly states, "not in my book. I chose to listen to Dr. Freeman. So, if that makes me scared, I'm cool with it."

Nasir, Khufu, and Robert are about to start arguing when Ahkhah walks in. "Good, we are all here."

"All here?" Robert concernedly asks.

"Yes, Khufu and Nasir have been sent to join us on the mission."

Robert looks suspicious. Who would send them? Why would they be sent?

"Good the more the merrier," Mischel excitingly says.

Khufu asks, "what exactly is the mission? We weren't told much."

"The Order wants to move a scroll to the United States. They believe it is now time. They were planning on doing it soon after the United States establishment but wanted to see how humans would react with the newly gained power.

It didn't take long for battles to occur between brothers of the same family. So, the order decided to hold off from moving the scrolls. In a final effort to awaken the people, this move is necessary."

Nasir states, "move a scroll to the UNITED SNAKES? It is a horrible place for African Americans. The scrolls must not be for us?"

"Have you ever lived in a totalitarian country like those in Africa?" Ahkhah inquires.

Nasir humbly responds, "NO."

"Are you allowed to speak against the bad treatment of African Americans or even the terrible job your president has done in your country?"

"Yes."

"In a totalitarian country, you will
end up in jail or dead for speaking
out. Think about that."

No one says a word quietly sitting
and waiting for further instructions
from Ahkhah.

Ahkhah continues, "the Order gave
the United States' founding fathers
knowledge of several sacred sciences of
the universe. Some of them thought it
was too dangerous to pass on to the
uninitiated. They hid the information
in their Mason group."

"Is this the same for the black
Masons?"

"No."

"But they are in the same group."

"They are the same group by name and
a few teachings. The explanation of the
universal principles was not shared
with the black Masons." Ahkhah looks at
his watch like a man on a mission. "It
is time to go. This trip shouldn't take
more than a day. There are two cars
outside waiting for us. From there we
will take a helicopter to the city of
Puebla. We will get into another car
that will drive us to Cholula."

Khufu asks, "isn't that where the pyramids are?"

"Yes."

They get into the cars. They eventually arrive in the town, a little tired but show much excitement, seeing the pyramid from their location.

Mischel is in awe, "this is beautiful."

"I must leave you, at this point," Ahkhah informs them.

Mischel is worried. "Leave us. What do you mean? I thought this was all of our journeys to finish Dr. Freeman's mission."

Khufu and Nasir look at each other in disgust. The name Dr. Freeman triggers a sick feeling in their stomachs. Cue talked so badly about him that Khufu and Nasir hate him.

"I am only here to assist. I have not been prepared for this mission. I am not allowed to witness what happens."

Khufu, Nasir, Mischel, and Robert looked confused, unprepared, or so they think.

"I know it does not make sense. I wish I could go with you, but I'll be waiting here for your return." Ahkhah pulls a piece of paper from his pocket with an enigma for the entrance into the pyramid. "I have only one question I must ask you. You are not to give me the answer. However, you must answer it before entering the pyramid. I suggest that you walk and talk with each other.

The question is: what do you need to make the journey? Now go and have a safe journey, I'll be waiting here."

They walk away from Ahkhah. Each of them is looking a little confused. Why do they have to go inside the pyramid?

Khufu and Nasir begin talking to each other.

Robert asks, "are we working together?"

Nasir quickly says, "you and your girlfriend can work together, and we'll work together."

"I'm not his girlfriend."

"You're not ours either. We do not know or trust you."

Mischel is upset. She feels disrespected.

Nasir continues, "may the best man, I mean people, win."

"Fine, yes, we will win," Mischel challenges.

They walk closer to the pyramid.

Khufu says to Nasir, "we need two flashlights, two knives, two guns for our protection, two backpacks, some rope, a first aid kit, a map of the inside. Can you think of anything else?"

"Some food."

Khufu laughs, "man, you're always hungry."

They see a vendor's tent near the entrance. Mysteriously, all the supplies Khufu and Nasir mentioned are there. A man gives it to them. They are ready.

Mischel and Robert notice a woman selling bread. Robert buys a piece to support the woman, still grateful for receiving some of the finest quality clothes for free. The woman smiles and gently hands it to him. He takes it, and for a good gesture, he bites into it and then collapses.

Khufu and Nasir look at him shaking their heads.

Nasir states, "he is still stupid."

Mischel, in a slight panic, asks, "aren't you going to help your friend?"

"He means nothing to us. He is a traitor. You take care of the idiot," Nasir viciously responds.

Mischel cradles Robert as he lays on the ground breathing heavily. She yells for help, but no one pays her any attention.

Khufu and Nasir walk towards the pyramid. They arrive at it, not knowing where the entrance is, they rub their hands across the stones attempting to locate it.

Robert, seemingly unconscious, has a vision. A flash shines. He sees Benjamin Franklin and the man who gave him the clothes standing together. Lightening hits his kite as electricity travels down the string, hitting the golden key, transforming into a white powder.

The older woman who sold him the bread gathers the powder. Some of the powder flies away as if it is anti-gravitational. She adds water to the remaining powder and presses it together in her hands. It looks like a tortilla. She offers it to Robert.

Suddenly Khufu and Nasir are sucked in the pyramid. Their equipment is heavy, pulling them down quickly. They fall several feet and hit the ground. Sand shoots up as they fell into a dust bowl.

They get up from the ground and wipe themselves off. Khufu asks, "are you alright?"

"Yeah, I'm good. What was that?"

"Your guess is as good as mines." Khufu gets his flashlight from inside the bag and continues to dig through it for the map. He finds it and pulls it out.

Nasir pulls his flashlight and gun out of his backpack.

They hear a voice, "this way to the prize."

They look at each other and nod, then follow the voice's instruction.

"Keep walking. Turn right here."

They turn right like the voice tells them.

"A few more steps, now make another right turn here."

They turn right like the voice tells them.

"Turn 180 degrees and enter the room."

They turn how the voice instructs and see a mysterious lit room. Khufu and Nasir enter the room with walls layered in gold and Egyptian hieroglyphics imprinted on the walls. In the center of the room is an altar with a golden chest on it.

Khufu runs to the chest. He looks closely. It has Egyptian hieroglyphics with a picture of Tehuti holding a papyrus and quill. "This must be it."

"Open it and see. If nothing is in it. It is not it. The voice misled us."

Khufu opens the chest filled with rolled-up papyruses. It looks too delicate for Khufu to unroll. "This has to be it."

"Cool, let's get out of this creepy place."

Khufu tries to lift the golden chest. It is heavy. He waves Nasir over to help him. They both grab a handle and lift it. As the chest leaves the altar, the pyramid begins to shake.

They attempt to run with the awkward chest, but it is too heavy, so they walk fast instead. The ceiling and walls begin to crumble. One wall falls, causing the rest of the room to fall towards them.

They panic, duck, and close their eyes, the noise stops, and they open their eyes, realizing that they are outside of the pyramid. They look at each other, confused. Then they look in the direction of the vendor's tent, which is no longer there.

They see Mischel, still cradling Robert, rocking him back and forth. She does not see Khufu and Nasir.

They sneak passed her and walk back to the car. They see Ahkhah as he nods at them. They get into the car and head for the border.

Nasir pulls out his cell phone. He dials Cue. "We got it."

"Good, hold on let me call our connection for further instruction." Cue dials a number and comes back so Nasir can hear the conversation.

A man answers the phone, "hello."

"Hey, just calling you to tell you that my men got the package."

"Good, when they get to the private airport my boss' private jet will be waiting there for them to bring them to us. We will pay you nicely for the job well done."

"I told you my men wouldn't fail."

"Yes, you did, thank you," the man hangs up the phone.

"General Nasir, you and Khufu definitely earned a promotion. You heard him. Get it to him safely. And we'll be set for life."

"Yessir."

They hang up the phone.

George is at a golf range. "They got the scrolls."

George's boss replies, "good, the scrolls will be in the best hands which YAHWEH has created."

CHAPTER 17

Robert eventually regains consciousness, looking around, he rubs his head in confusion as Mischel gently holds his head. As he gets up, he staggers, feeling an unexplained emotion.

Mischel watches as he stands. "Are you ok?"

"Yeah I'm fine."

Mischel tearfully says, "You had me scared. No one would help me."

"Thank you for making sure I was alright. I owe you."

"You're right about that. You owe me big. Your friends left us."

"That is cool. We are probably better off without them."

"What happened?"

"That bread knocked me out, but I saw something amazing."

"What did you see because I saw something earlier?"

"We can talk about it later. Let's get into this pyramid. What do you think we need?"

"Nothing. I have faith in the creative force. We will be alright."

"I agree. Let's go. Do you want to hold hands as we enter?" Robert was testing what he felt.

"Yes."

They grab hands. They slowly walk towards the pyramid. Instead of trying to force their way in, they look at each other. Mischel closes her eyes. Robert follows and closes his eyes.

An energy force gently pulls them inside. The entire inside of the pyramid is lit, unlike Khufu and Nasir experienced.

A powerful voice says, "your faith is in the right place. You have passed. Proceed into the room on your right side."

They enter the room. The walls are gold with hieroglyphics imprinted on them. An altar sits in the center of the room with a golden chest on it.

They are startled when 13 people enter the room. There are 7 women and 6 men. They circle them.

They are wearing all black. They dawn a black tarboosh with a half-moon over two triangles. One is upside down, and the other is right-side up. They would be touching at the point, but a circle is in between the two points. Under the upright triangle is a sword. The top triangle has a 6-pointed star in it. Inside the bottom triangle, there sits a 5-pointed star.

All of them except for one woman have aprons on with the same emblem. The woman is wearing a golden sash and a golden cape. Her skin is a glowing golden-brown complexion. Her hair is silky white. She has deep wrinkles in her face and hands. She steps forward, "Welcome."

Mischel and Robert stand silently, not knowing what to do. They wait for further instruction.

Two spirits shaped like humans enter the room. One of them is Dr. Freeman. "We, the keepers of the temple, congratulate you both for making it to this point. It was a long journey, but my faith in the two of you proved you to be the chosen ones." He points at the other spirit. "This is GRAND MASTER RUSSELL TURNER of the spiritual form. Robert, this is your grandfather, Rusty."

Robert is stun, remembering magnificent stories about the adventures of his grandfather RUSSELL TURNER. His grandfather disappeared on a mission.

Russell, bringing his right hand to his chest, begins to speak. His voice sounds like running water. "It is good to see you again, son. I am glad you made it. You have been named perfectly to enter our Order."

"Mischel, you have a family member here too." Dr. Freeman points to the woman wearing the sash, "she is your father's aunt. Her name is SESHET ZIAD. She is the Grand Master in the physical form. Your family has also been a part of our great order for centuries."

Mischel grabs her heart because she is surprised. She never met any family member on his side of the family. Mischel only dreamed of one-day meeting one of them. She stands in gratitude to finally meet one of her family members.

Seshet walks to Mischel and hugs her, kissing her on her forehead. Then she walks back to her position. "Welcome to the Temple of Mystery. For our GREAT ORDER to continue, we must pass the ancient knowledge to those found worthy. Are the two of you willing to receive it?"

Mischel and Robert both say, "Yes."

"Excellent, who wants to go first?"

"Ladies first," Robert looks at Mischel and smiles.

Mischel smiles and raises her hand.

"Come up to the altar my dear child. Place both hands on the altar."

Mischel does as instructed. The 15 members beam a green light into her forehead. It takes about one minute.

Seshet further instructs, "green represents healing. Take a step back."

The altar lowers into the ground. Then the 15 members beam a gold light into her solar plexus. It takes about 2 minutes. Seshet waves for Mischel to join the circle standing next to her.

The altar rises back up. Russell states, "Robert, my son, you are next. Walk to the altar. Place both hands on the chest."

Robert follows the instructions. The 15 members beam the gold light for about a minute into his forehead, opposite of Mischel.

"Gold represents knowledge. Turn around."

The altar lowers, and the 15 members beam the green light into his solar plexus for about 3 minutes.

"You are both a part of our GREAT ORDER. The last instruction for both of you is to close your eyes," Russell announces.

Mischel and Robert close their eyes. They feel a cool breeze like they are floating.

They hear a whisper say, "Open your eyes."

They are outside of the pyramid and look at each other, then hug, as they stand admiring the pyramid and the surroundings.

"So, are you going to tell me what you saw when you were unconscious?"

"I think we will have a lifetime to talk about it. Let's just enjoy each other and reflect on our experience."

Mischel lovingly grabs his hand. They shared something special. They walk towards Ahkhah, who patiently waits for them.

Ahkhah, "are you ready to leave?"

Mischel worryingly looks at Robert, "Robert, we didn't get the scroll."

They both look at Ahkhah.

"You will get the scroll in time," Ahkhah comforts them.

Mischel then asks, "what about Khufu and Nasir? Are we going to leave them?"

Ahkhah responds, "they are already taken care of."

Mischel and Robert continue to hold hands.

They all walk to the car and drive off.

CHAPTER 18

Khufu and Nasir get out at the border. They have a cab waiting on the other side to take them to the airport. They walk ready to cross the border with the gold chest.

The Border Patrol officer stops them. "what's this?"

Khufu responds, "it is a chest we bought from a local

"It looks mighty expensive. You say you bought it from a vendor? Do you have any paper showing you bought it?"

Nasir, slightly nervous, says, "no sir, we didn't think we'd need any." He realizes that they might have a problem.

"For something like this you need it. Set it down here and follow me."

"We'd rather take it with us. It has all our valuables in it," Nasir says.

"It will be safe here. I'm not going to ask you a second time."

They put the chest down and follow the Border Officer. Immediately, the officer arrests them for trying to take contraband across the border.

A janitor walks in the room where the chest sits. It looks like a paper box to him, never seeing it there before, he picks it up as if it is light as a feather and takes it to the incinerator. He throws it in as purple smoke comes from it. He stands and watches it burn to ashes.